REINCARNATIONS

REINCARNATIONS

HARRY TURTLEDOVE

FOUNTAINDALE PUBLIC LIBRARY

300 West Briarcliff Road
Bolingbrook, IL 60440-2894
(630)   759-2102

WSFA Press

REINCARNATIONS

WSFA Press
www.wsfapress.com

Trade Hardcover ISBN: 978-0-9621725-6-4
Limited Edition ISBN: 978-0-9621725-7-1

TABLE OF CONTENTS

INTRODUCTION
by Sheila Williams

THERE ARE A COUPLE OF IMPORTANT POINTS I'D LIKE TO make about Harry Turtledove. One point that anyone who has read Harry's work knows is that he's a terrific writer. My own opinion of Harry's work was formed by two stories from the mid-eighties. I read each tale in galleys before its publication in *Asimov's*. Although they inhabited alternate universes and were separated in time from my own experience, I found the powerful and realistic writing deeply convincing and affecting.

"Strange Eruptions" appeared in *Asimov's* August 1986 issue. Making use of his doctorate in Byzantine history, Harry sets it in a fourteenth century Constantinople that is capital of a Byzantine Empire that never fell. Both the historical detail and the depiction of a devastating smallpox epidemic are utterly convincing. What seemed most realistic, though, were the actions of the characters—the wife who insists on attending Mass surrounded by people in the great church of Hagia Sophia in order to pray that her family be spared from the disease, the husband who awkwardly attempts to nurse his small baby through the child's horrible illness. The emotional toll that the disease took on the survivors still resonates with me.

The other story, "Trapping Run," appeared in the February 1989 issue of *Asimov's*. The tale is part of an alternate world in which European explorers discover that *Homo erectus,* or "sims," and not Native Americans, inhabit the New World. The story tells the tale of a trapper whose leg is shattered by a bear. His only hope of survival is to be cared for by the "subhuman" sims. It's one of the most brutal and realistic depictions of injury and endurance that I have ever come across. It remains a gold standard for judging other tales in which authors present characters that survive against all odds.

Both stories were collected into books that I worked on— *Agent of Byzantium* and *A Different Flesh*—for a short-lived book-publishing venture. These volumes were later reprinted by Baen Books.

Alas, as Harry turned more to writing his original and inventive novels, his short fiction output seemed to slow down. From time to time, though, works, both funny and hard hitting, continued to show up at the magazines. In 1999, Harry conducted an interesting experiment. He sold a story to *Asimov's* entitled "Forty, Counting Down," about a time-traveler who revisits his past in order help his younger self. At the same time (and with the full knowledge of both editors) he sold another story to *Analog,* "Forty, Counting Up," from the point of view of the young man who receives a visit from his older self.

Although his work is often suffused with good humor, Harry has continued to write uncompromising stories that deftly explore the human condition. A perfect example of one of these thought-provoking tales, "He Woke in Darkness," is included in this collection. It was the first story that I, as editor of *Asimov's,* had the chance to publish. This disturbing look at crime and punishment and human behavior is one that readers will not soon forget.

So, I've established that Harry is a terrific writer, but there is a second point that I would like to make as well. Harry is also a delightful person with a wonderful family. I have often traveled to science fiction conventions with my own family in tow, and I have learned that there are not too many writers upon whom I can safely inflict a young child's companionship. In many cases, my husband and children are packed off to a museum or a zoo while I dine with my Hugo or Nebula nominee. There are times, though, when an entire weekend spent working at a convention does not allow me to escape all my obligations as a mother. If I intend to do my job and have a meal with my children, I have to make a date with a child friendly author. Harry and his family are high on that very short list. He and his delightful wife, Laura Frankos, along with their smart, witty, and lovely daughters, Alison, Rachel, and Rebecca, are experts at making small children feel like their opinions are valuable, too. Now that my oldest daughter is a teenager, she fondly recalls meals spent with the Turtledoves. She also wows her friends—several of whom are avid Harry Turtledove readers—when she tells them that she knows him. Harry can count two generations of my family among his thousands of readers. Since you're holding this book right now, I'm glad that you are, or will soon be, one of those lucky readers, too.

THE HAUNTED BICUSPID

This one first appeared in *The Enchanter Completed*, the tribute anthology to L. Sprague de Camp that I had the privilege of editing. Being a tavern tale, it's a sort of *hommage* to de Camp and Pratt's classic *Tales from Gavagan's Bar*. That's why the bartender here is called "George M." You're supposed to think "Cohan," the name of de Camp and Pratt's barkeep. As for the rest, well, I had the chance to be a Poe-t, and I took it.

HERE'S TWO DOLLARS AND FIFTY CENTS—IN GOLD, BY God, George M. A quarter-eagle's plenty to buy drinks for every body in the place. Tell me when you need more. I'll do it again.

What's that you say, my friend? You see more gold now than you did just a few years ago? Well, I should hope you do, by thunder. It's all coming from California, way out West. I don't suppose any one would have thought the world held so much gold until they stumbled across it on that Sutter fellow's land.

But I don't feel like talking about gold right this here minute—except that that's *my* gold on the bar. If I'm buying, part of what I'm buying is the chance to talk about any blamed thing I please. Any body feel like quarreling about that?

No? Good.

All right, then. Here goes. Friends, my name is William Legrand. Most of you know me, and most of you call me Bill. I'm a plain-spoken man, I am. Nothing fancy about me. Yes, I'm partial to canvasback duck and soft-shell crabs when I can get 'em, but what Baltimorean isn't? That's not fancy—they're right good eating, and who'll tell me they aren't?

I was born in the year of our Lord 1800. Last year of the eighteenth century, that was, and don't you believe any silly fool who tries to tell you it was the first year of the nineteenth. As of the twenty-seventh *ultimo*, that makes me a right round fifty-one years of age. I am not ashamed to say I have done pretty well for myself in that half century and a little bit. If there's a single soul who sells more furniture or finer furniture in Baltimore, I'd like to know who he is. Helen and I have been married for twenty-eight years now, and we still get on better than tolerably well. I have three sons and a daughter, and Helen was lucky enough never to lose a baby, for which I thank God. One of my sons went to Harvard, another to Yale. I wasn't able to do that kind of thing myself, but a man's children should have more chances than he did. That's the American way, don't you think? And I have two little granddaughters now, and I wouldn't trade 'em for anything. Not for the moon, do you hear me?

If it weren't for my teeth, everything would be perfect.

I see some of you wince. I see some of you flinch. I see I am not the only man in this splendid establishment to find himself a martyr to the tooth-ache. I am not surprised to make that discovery. People laugh about the tooth-ache—people who haven't got it laugh at it, I should say. And Old Scratch is welcome to every single one of those laughing hyenas.

I was still a young man the first time I faced the gum lancet, the punch, the pincers, the lever, and the pelican. They sound like tools for an old-time torturer, don't they? By God, gentlemen, they *are* tools for an old-time torturer. Any of you who ever had dealings with a dentist more than a few years ago will know what I am talking about. Oh, yes, I see some heads going up and down. I knew I would.

Here's another quarter-eagle, George M. You keep that river flowing for these gentlemen, if you would be so kind.

People would say, You try this, Bill, or, You do that, Bill, and it will not hurt so bad. I would drink myself blind before I went to have a tooth yanked. Or I would take so much opium, I could not even recollect my own name. Or I would do both those things at once, so that my friends would have to steer me to the latest butcher because I could not navigate on my own.

And when the damned quack got to work, whoever he was that time, it would hurt worse than anything you can think of. If he grabs a tooth with the pincers, and instead of pulling it he breaks it, and he has to jerk out all the fragments one at a time, what else is it going to do? I ask you, my friends, what else can it *possibly* do?

I tell you frankly, I was more relieved than sorry when I lost the last tooth down below—ten years ago it was now. My bottom false teeth fit tolerably well, and I don't mind 'em a bit. But I wanted to hang on to the ones I have up top. I still do want that, as a matter of fact. If you have a full plate up there, they hold in your uppers with springs, and that is another infernal invention. There are plenty of ways I would like to be like George Washington, but that is not one of them.

But God does what He wants, not what you want. Not what I want, either. About six months ago, it was, when one of my top left bicuspids went off like it had a fire lit inside it.

What's a bicuspid? On each side, top and bottom, you have got two teeth betwixt your eyeteeth and your grinders. Ask a dentist, and he will tell you they're bicuspids. I have done a powerful lot of palavering with dentists over the years. I know how they talk. I am a man who likes to learn things. I want to find out just precisely what they are going to inflict on me before they go and inflict it.

And a whole fat lot of good *that* has done me, too.

I kept hoping the tooth-ache would go away. Might as well hope the bill collector or your mother-in-law will go away. You stand a better chance. Before long, I knew it was time to get me to a dentist—that or go plumb out of my mind. I had not had to lose a chopper for five or six years before that. The last quack I had gone to was out of business. Maybe the folks he tormented strung him up. I can hope so, anyhow.

So I found me another fellow, a Dutchman named Vankirk. He grinned when he saw my poor sorry mouth. *His* teeth, damn him, were as white as if he soaked 'em in cat piss every night. For all I know, maybe he did.

He poked at my poor sore chopper with one of those iron hooks his miserable tribe uses. You know the type I mean—like out of the Spanish Inquisition, only smaller. He had to pry me off the ceiling afterwards, too. You bet he did. Then he gave me another shiny smile. "Oh, yes, Mr. Legrand," he says, "I can have that out in jig time, and a replacement in the socket, and you will not feel a thing."

I laughed in his face. "Go peddle your papers," I says. "I am not a blushing bride at this business. I have been with your kind of man before. I have heard promises like that before. I have stupefied myself with every remedy known to nature. And it has hurt like blazes every single time."

"Every remedy known to nature, perhaps," says Vankirk. "But what about remedies known to man? Have you ever visited a dentist who uses chloroform?"

Now, I had heard of his stuff. It was written up in the *Baltimore Sun* not so long before. But, "Just another humbug," says I.

Vankirk shook his head. "Mr. Legrand, chloroform is no humbug," he says, solemn as a preacher at a millionaire's funeral. "They can take off a man's leg with it—never mind his tooth, his *leg*—and he will not feel a thing until he wakes up. I have been using it for six months, and it is a sockdolager."

In my day, I have been lied to by a good many dentists. I am familiar with the breed. If this Vankirk was lying, he was better at it than any other tooth-drawer I have had the displeasure to know. I felt something I had not felt since my very first acquaintance with the pincers. Friends, I felt hope.

"You can pop a replacement tooth in when you yank mine, you say?" I ask him. "I have had that done before, more than once, and never known it to hold above a year."

"Plainly, you have been visiting men who do not know their business," says Vankirk. "From examining your mouth, I believe I have the very tooth that will make a perfect fit in your jaw."

He opened a drawer and rummaged in a box of teeth and finally found the one he wanted. It looked like a tooth to me. That is all I can tell you. It did not have blood and pus all over it, I will say that, the way mine do when one butcher or another hauls them out of my jaw. I ask him, "Where did it come from?"

"Out of the mouth of a brave young soldier killed at the battle of Buena Vista," Vankirk says. "This tooth, Mr. Legrand, is good for twenty or thirty more years than you are. You may count on that."

I never count on anything a dentist tells me. I say, "In my day, I have had teeth put in my head from men slain in the War of 1812, the Black Hawk War, and the war the Texans fought against Mexico before the US of A decided to teach Santa Anna a lesson. Not a one of them lasted. Why should I think this here one will be any different?"

"It is not the tooth alone, Mr. Legrand. It is the man who puts it in," he says, and strikes a pose.

He did not lack for confidence, Vankirk. And the one I had in there had to come out. I knew that. I would not have been there if I didn't. But, says I, "Tell me one thing—is this here tooth an American's or a Mexican's?"

"An American's," he answers right away. He was all set to get shirty about it, too. "Do you think I would stick a damned greaser's tooth in your jaw? No, sir."

"That was what I wanted to know," I say, and I sat down in his chair. "Go ahead, then. Let us get it over with."

George M., I see there are folks with empty glasses. Why don't you keep them filled? We can settle the score when I am done. You know me. I am good for it. If I am not, no man in Baltimore is. Thank you kindly, sir. You are a gentleman, as I have cause to know.

Where was I? Oh, yes—in that blamed dentist's chair. Says I, "Won't you strap down my arms so I can't punch you while you are pulling?"

"No need. I was not lying when I said it would not hurt," Vankirk says. He opened that drawer again, the one the tooth came out of. This time, he had hold of a bottle and a rag. He soaked the rag in the stuff in the bottle—it looked like water—but it wasn't—and then he hauled off and stuck that wet rag over my nose and mouth.

The chloroform—that was what it had to be, chloroform—smelled sweet and nasty at the same time. It did not smell like anything I had ever known before. When I opened my mouth to yell, it tasted sweet, too. It tasted *unnaturally* sweet, to tell you the truth. It tasted *so* sweet, it burned.

What I meant for that yell came out like a gurgle. It was like all of a sudden I was drunker than I had ever been before. Well, no. It was not *just* like that, you understand. But it was closer to that than to anything else you will know if you have not been under chloroform yourself. And then I was not drunk any more. I was *gone*.

When I woke up, at first I did not realize I was waking up. I did not know I had been asleep, you see. My senses were still reeling. I started to ask Vankirk when he was going to start. That was when I realized my mouth tasted all bloody.

I also realized I could not talk, not for hell. I wondered if the chloroform had scrambled my brains for fair. But it was not the chloroform. Vankirk had stuffed a wad of cloth in there to soak up some of the blood. I spat it out, and did not land it on my breeches, for which I was grateful.

Says I, "This *is* no humbug. It did not hurt."

"No, sir," Vankirk says. He held up his pincers. In it, he still had the black ruin that was my tooth. Its bottom end was all smeared with blood, like I knew it would be. He took it out of the pincers and flung it in the rubbish. "No use putting this old ruin in another man's head."

"I reckon not," says I.

"The one I put there in its place fit as though it was made there," Vankirk says. "I have been doing this for a while now, Mr. Legrand, and I have never had a transplanted tooth go in so well."

"Good," says I. I felt around with my tongue. Sure enough, the new tooth was in there. It was fixed to the one in back of it by fine wire. Not to the one in front. That there one is long gone.

Vankirk says, "You will feel some pain now, as the chloroform wears off. You see, I do not lie to you. Have you got some laudanum with you?"

"That I do," I says, and I took a few drops. I know about the pain after a tooth comes out. I ought to. It is not so bad. Laudanum—which is opium in brandy, for any one who does not know—laudanum, I say, can shift that pain all right.

"As your jaw heals, that tooth will become a part of you," Vankirk says. "Because it fit in there so exceedingly well, I think it will last a long time."

Like I said, friends, I have had teeth transplanted before. Not a one of them stayed in place long. I had said as much to the tooth-drawer. I started to say so again. But then I shut my mouth, and not on account of I was still bleeding some. He knew what he was talking about with the chloroform. Maybe he knew what he was talking about here, too.

"Can you walk?" he asks me. "Are you all right to go?"

I got to my feet. The room swayed some, but it was not too bad. I have felt drunker than I did just then. "I am fine, thank you," says I. "And I *do* thank you—believe me, I do." I think this was the first time I ever thanked a tooth-drawer after escaping his clutches. I confess, though, I may be mistaken. Now and then, I have been suffering sufficient so as to thank one of those brigands no matter what he did to me.

"Walk around my room here a bit. I want to make certain

you are steady on your pins," Vankirk says. So I did that. It was not too bad. On my third or fourth circuit, I caught the dentist's eye. He nodded, for I had satisfied him. Says he, "Come back in a fortnight. I will take the wire off that new tooth I put in there. It should do fine on its own. With any luck at all, it will last you the rest of your life."

"I will do just as you say. Let us make the appointment now," I answer him. So we did. He wrote it in a book he had, and he wrote it for me on a scrap of paper. I put that in my waistcoat pocket. "And after that," says I, and I planted my beaver hat on my head, "you will see me nevermore."

Looking back, I do believe that to be the very commencement of my troubles, the beginning of a descent into the maelstrom from which I was fortunate in the extreme to escape unscathed, or nearly so. But at this time I knew nothing of what lay ahead, nothing of the ordeal to which I was to be subjected.

My head still whirled a bit from the chloroform and from the laudanum. I could walk, however, and knew where I was going. And I was leaving the dentist's, and it did not hurt. *It did not hurt.* Since the Passion and Resurrection of our Lord, I do not think God has wrought a greater miracle.

When I returned to my house, Helen flew into my arms. "Oh, Bill! Poor Bill!" she cried. "How are you, you sorry, abused creature?"

"I am—well enough," I answered, and regaled her with the tale of my experience. As she hearkened to the story, her eyes, the outward expression of her soul, grew ever wider in astonishment. Kissing her tenderly yet carefully, I continued,

"And so you see, my dear, I am in a state to be envied rather than pitied."

"No one who loses a tooth is to be envied," she said, which is true enough, "but I am gladder than I can express that it was not the torment you have known too many times."

"So am I, by all that is holy," I replied. "He told me the chloroform was no humbug, and he told me the truth. Who would have expected such a thing from a dentist?"

My three sons, my daughter, and her husband, knowing I was to be subjected to this latest bout of toothly torment, came to call upon me in turn to learn how I was, and were pleasantly amazed to discover me so well. I am, as I have previously observed, fortunate in my family.

They all exclaimed to no small degree on observing me to be free of the agonies I had hitherto endured during and subsequent to the forced removal of that which Nature purposed to endure for ever. And Benjamin, my eldest, on learning in full what had transpired, said, "So you have another man's tooth in your jaw in place of your own?"

"I do indeed," I replied.

"And from what unlucky soul came the mortal fragment?" he inquired.

"Why, from a fallen hero of the late war against Mexico," I informed him. "So, at any rate, said Mr. Vankirk. He seeming otherwise veracious, I have no cause to doubt his word—But why do you laugh? What have I said or done to inspire such mirth?"

"You will know, dear and loving Father," said Benjamin, "that my particular friend is Dr. Ernest Valdemar, with whom

I studied at Harvard College. Owing to your dental miseries, we have found occasions too numerous to mention on which to discuss such matters. He has, generally speaking, a low opinion of transplanted teeth."

"As has Mr. Vankirk, generally speaking," I replied. "*Exceptio probat regulam*, however, and he believed I would do well with this new tooth inserted into my jaw. Since he spoke the truth—indeed, if anything, less than the truth—regarding the analgesic and anaesthetic properties of chloroform, I see no reason not to hope, at least, he likewise had cause to be sanguine about my long-continuing use of a tooth now valueless to the soldier who once bore it."

He held up a hand to forestall my further speech, and then declared, "Dr. Valdemar has also a low opinion of those who gather these bits of ivory for the tooth-drawers' trade—harvesters, he styles them. He says, and he should be in a position to know, that the bulk of the teeth employed in dentures and in transplantation come not from battlefields but from graveyards and even from the potter's field, stolen at night in the dark of the moon by those whose deeds must not see the light of day. Whose tooth, then, Father, dwells now in that socket once your own?"

I will not—I cannot—deny the *frisson* of horror and dread shooting through me at this question. If the donor of the dental appendage was not the stalwart soldier to whom Vankirk had animadverted, who was he? Who, indeed? Some fiend in human shape? Some nameless, useless, worthless scribbler, his brief, strutting time on earth all squandered, his soul gone to fearful judgement, and his fleshly envelope flung now into a pauper's grave?

My laugh holding more heartiness than I truly felt, I essayed to make light of my beloved Benjamin's apprehensions. "In a fortnight's time, I shall see Vankirk again; it is then he will remove the wire affixing the new tooth to its neighbor, that neighbor being one of the handful of sound instruments of mastication remaining in my upper mandible," I said. "That will be time enough to discuss the matter with him, and, I pledge to you, I shall not omit doing so."

Setting a kindly hand upon my shoulder, my eldest said, "Let it be as you wish, then, Father. My concern is only for you; I would not have you—contaminated by some unclean bit of matter rightfully residing on the far side of the tomb."

My own chief concern after receipt of the new tooth was not contamination but suppuration, the almost inevitable bout of pus and fever attendant upon such rude intrusions upon the oral cavity as the tooth-drawer is compelled to make. Having suffered several such bouts—having, indeed, lost a cousin at an untimely age as a result of one—I knew the signs, and awaited them with the apprehension to be expected from a man of such knowledge. Yet all remained well, and, in fact, I healed with a rapidity hardly less astonishing to me than the anodyne of chloroform itself. By the third day after the extraction, I was up and about and very largely my usual self once more.

Fourteen days having passed, I repaired to the illustrious Vankirk's so that he might examine the results of his ministrations upon me. "Good-morning, Mr. Legrand," he said. "How fare you to-day?"

"Exceeding well; monstrous well, you might even say," I replied. "Undo your wire, sir, and I shall be on my way."

"If the socket be healed sufficiently, I shall do just as you say. In the meantime"—here gesturing towards the chair whence I had been fortunate enough to make my escape half a month before—"take a seat, if you would be so kind."

"I am entirely at your service," I said, reflecting as I sat upon how great a prodigy it was that one such as I, with my fear both morbid and well-earned of those practicing the dentist's art, should allow such a pronouncement to pass his lips as any thing save the most *macabre* jest.

A tiny, sharp-nosed plier of shiny iron in his hand, Vankirk bent towards me—and I, I willingly opened my mouth. "Well, well," quoth he, commencing his work, "here is a thing most extraordinary."

"What is it?" I enquired—indistinctly, I fear me, on account of the interference with my ejaculation arising from his hand and instrument.

First removing the wire, as he had told me he would, he answered, "Why, how very well you have recovered from your ordeal, Mr. Legrand, and how perfectly the tooth I have transplanted into your jawbone has taken hold there. If I—if any man—could do such work with every patient, I would serve kings, and live as kings do; for kings are no less immune to the tooth-ache than any other mortals."

"You did better with me than I had dreamt possible, Mr. Vankirk, and should I again stand in need of the services of a tooth-drawer—which, given the way of all flesh, and of my sorry flesh in especial, strikes me as being altogether too probable— you may rest assured I shall hasten hither to your establishment as quickly as ever I may; for, rendered insensible by the miracle of chloroform, I shall at last be able—or rather, happily unable—to cry out, imitating the famous and goodly Paul long ago in his first letter to the Corinthians, 'O pincers, where is thy sting? O torment, where is thy victory?' and knowing myself to have triumphed over the agonies that have tortured mankind for ever and ever."

Still holding the pliers, Vankirk cocked his head to one side, examining me with a keenness most disconcerting. After a moment, he shook his head, a quizzical expression playing across his countenance. "Extraordinary indeed," he murmured.

"Why say you that, sir, when I—?"

I had scarcely begun the question ere the tooth-drawer raised a hand, quelling my utterance before it could be well born. "Extraordinary in that you are, to all appearances, a changed man," he said.

"Why, so I am—I am a man free from pain, for which I shall remain ever in your debt, figuratively if not financially," I said.

"Our financial arrangements are satisfactory in the highest degree," Vankirk said. "By every account reaching my ear, you are and have always been a man of the nicest scrupulosity in respect to money, and in this you seem to have altered not by the smallest jot or tittle; not even by the proverbial iota, smaller than either. But your present style—how shall I say it?—differs somewhat from that which I observed in you a fortnight previously. And, as the illustrious Buffon (not to be confused with any of our present illustrious buffoons) so justly remarked, '*Le style c'est l'homme même.*' I trust you would agree?"

"How could any man disagree with such a sage observation?" I returned. "As an apologia, however, I must remind you that my faculties at the time of our last encounter were more than a little deranged by the pain of which you so skillfully relieved me."

"It could be," he replied, studying me with even greater keenness than before. "Yes, it could be. Yet the transformation seems too striking for that to be the sole fount wherefrom it arises."

"I know none other, unless"—and I laughed; yes, laughed! fool that I was—"you would include in your calculations the tooth of which you made me a gift in exchange for my own dear, departed bicuspid. Tell me, if you would—what is the tooth's true origin? Some source closer than a sanguinary field from the late war with Mexico? Am I correct in guessing you obtained it from some local—harvester, I believe the term is?"

"Well—since from some source or another—"

"My eldest son, whose particular friend is a doctor."

"I see. Since you have learned the term from your son, then, I shall not deny the brute fact of the matter. Yes, you have a Baltimore tooth, not one from the Mexican War. But I insist, Mr. Legrand, that it is a tooth as sound as I declared it to be when first I showed it to you, the truth of which is demonstrated by the rapidity and thoroughness with which it has incorporated itself into the matrix of your dentition. That last you cannot possibly deny."

"Nor would I attempt to do so," I replied, rising from the chair in which I had, on this occasion, neither suffered the tortures inflicted upon those condemned to the nether regions by the just judgement of the Almighty nor experienced the miracle of complete insensibility granted through the agency of the dentist's chloroform, but merely undergone some tiny and transitory discomfort whilst Vankirk removed the wire tethering the transplanted tooth to its natural neighbor. "Truly, I have a better opinion of you after your frank and manly admission of the facts of the matter than I would have had as the result of some vain and pompous effort at dissembling."

Vankirk scraped a match against the sole of his shoe to light a cigarillo; the sulfurous stink springing from the combustion of the match head warred briefly with the tobacco's sweeter smoke before failing, just as the Opponent of all that is good, he who dwells in brimstone, shall surely fail at the end of days. Pausing after his first inhalation, he said, "Your style has indeed undergone an alteration; and what this portends, and whether it be for good or ill, I know not—and, I believe, only the sequential unfolding of the leaves of the Book of Time shall hold the answer."

"I am but a man; a featherless biped, as the divine Plato put it; though not, I should hope, Voltaire the cynic's plucked chicken; and, as a man, I can only agree that the future is unknowable until it shall have become first present and then past; while, as a man named William Legrand—commonly called Bill—I can only assert that no change perceptible to me other than the relief of my distress through your art has eventuated in the time that is now the recent past, this time being as impalpable as the future but, unlike it, perceptible through memory, whatever sort of spiritual or physical phenomenon memory may one day prove to be."

"God bless my soul," the tooth-drawer declared, and then, upon due reflection, "yes, and yours as well."

"Yes," I said, "and mine as well."

On leaving his place of business, I truly believed all would be well, or as well as it might be for one with my notorious dental difficulties. The only cloud appearing upon the horizon of my imagination was the fear—no, not really the fear; say rather, the concern—that the tooth transplanted to my maxilla, whencever it first came, would weaken and abandon its adopted home. This showed no sign of eventuating. Indeed, as day followed day that tooth became attached ever more firmly to my jaw. Would that my own had been so tenacious of adhesion to the jawbone from which they sprang.

For some considerable while, then, all seemed well. No—again I misstate the plain truth, which is that for some considerable while all *was* well. Not every thing was perfect; we speak of a man's life, after all, not an angel's. But all went as I would have hoped, or near enough. The most that occurred of an unusual—certainly not uncanny, not yet—nature was that one or two or perhaps even several individuals imitated Vankirk the tooth-drawer in remarking upon what they perceived as an alteration to my accustomed forms of speech.

"What ever can you mean?" I enquired of one of these, a newspaper man by the name of Thomas Bob. "I note no variation from my utterances of days gone by."

"Whether it be perceptible to yourself or not, your prolixity, I must tell you, has increased to a remarkable degree," Thomas Bob replied. "Were that not so, would I remark upon it?" He laughed immoderately; such were the jests of which he was enamored.

"My prolixity, say you? Why, am I not the same simple, straight-forward fellow I always was, a man to call a spade a spade, and not, with Tacitus, an implement for digging trenches—you will, I pray, forgive my failing to append the original Latin, which unfortunately I cannot at the moment—"

"Enough!" He committed the sin of interruption, sometimes merely a peccadillo of the most venial sort, but at others approaching the mortal. So I felt it to be now. This notwithstanding, my acquaintance continued, "Do you not see, Legrand, how far you have gone down the road towards proving my assertion?"

"No," I said—only this and nothing more.

Again, Thomas Bob gave forth with the heartiest expression of his mirth, which increased my liking for him, for a man who will laugh when the joke is on himself is more highly to be esteemed than one who either cannot imagine the possibility of such a thing or who at once is inspired at once to hatred on becoming the butt of another's wit. We parted on the friendliest terms. I asked him to convey my regards to his son, who has lately attained to prominence as an editor of magazines.

Several days after my meeting with this distinguished gentleman, I had a dream of such extraordinary clarity—indeed, of such verisimilitude—as to surpass any I had ever known before. Some of these, whether they spring from the lying gate of ivory or the true gate of horn to which Homer animadverts, are fonts of delight. Not so the one darkening my slumbers on the night I now describe.

I was black, to begin with. Now, I will not speak to the issue of whether the negro should by rights be slave or free; that is a discussion for another time and another place, and one that, the Compromise of 1850 notwithstanding, seems to be as likely to be decided by shot and shell as by the quills and quillets of fussy barristers. Suffice to say, the Legrands have not, nor have we ever had, the faintest tincture of colored blood flowing in our veins.

Yet I was black, black as soot, black as coal, black as ebony, black as India ink, black as midnight in a sky without stars or moon, black as Satan's soul. And, when I first came to myself in this dream, I found I was high amongst the branches of a great tulip-tree. Glancing down for even the briefest instant engendered terror which nearly sufficed to loose my grip upon the trunk and send be hurtling to my doom, as Lucifer hurtled from the heavens long, long ago.

Quickly gathering myself, I managed to hang on, and to climb. The branch upon which I was at length compelled to crawl shuddered under my weight, not least on account of its rotten state. Whoever would send any man, even a worthless negro, on such a mission deserves, in my view, nothing less than horsewhipping. Yet I had no choice; I *must* go forward, or face a fate even worse than the likelihood of plunging, screaming death.

Crawling on, I came upon a human skull spiked to the said branch (a skull with, as I noted enviously, teeth of an extraordinary whiteness and soundness; whatever had pained this mortal morsel, the dreaded tooth-ache had kept apart from his door). I dropped through one of the skull's gaping eye sockets a scarabaeous beetle of remarkable heft; it glinted of gold as it fell.

And then, as is the way of dreams, I found myself on the ground once more, digging at a spot chosen by extending a line from the center of the trunk through the spot where the beetle fell. Imagine my delight upon discovering a wooden chest banded with iron, of the sort in which pirates were wont to bury treasure. Imagine my despair upon discovering it to be full of—teeth.

Yes, teeth. Never had I seen such a marvelous profusion of dentality all gathered together at one and the same place. Incisors, eyeteeth, bicuspids, molars; so many, they might have been a flock of passenger pigeons turned to rooted enamel. Under the bright sun of my imagined sky, they shone almost as if they were the gold and jewels for which I had surely hoped.

I reached down and ran my hand through them. The not unpleasing music they made striking one against another suggested something to me, something not merely musical but reminding me of—Of what I never learned, for I awoke then, and the answer, if answer there was, vanished and was lost for ever, as is the way of dreams. Yet the dream itself remained perfect in my memory, suffering none of the usual distortion and diminution attendant upon these nocturnal visions in the clear light of morning.

A few nights later, I dreamt once more; once more I found myself in a world seeming perfectly real, yet assuredly the product of a dreadful and disordered imagination. My enemies—vile ecclesiastics of some inquisitorial sect better left unnamed—had captured me and condemned me to a death of cruelty unparalleled, a death wherein the horror of anticipation only added to the innate terror of extinction lodged in the breast of brute beast and man alike.

I lay on my back, strapped to a low wooden platform by the securest of leather lashings, at the bottom of a deep and but dimly lighted chamber. And above me—as yet some distance above me, but slowly and inexorably lowering towards my helpless and recumbent frame—swung an immense pendulum, hissing through the air at its every passage. The heavy metal ball weighting it would have sufficed—would far more than have sufficed—to crush the life from me when its arc should at last have met my yielding flesh, but that, apparently, was not the doom ordained for me.

For, you see, affixed to the bottom of the weighty ball was an enormous *tooth*, sharpened by patient and cunning art until its cutting edge glittered with a keenness to which the patient swordsmiths who shaped blades from finest Damascus steel might only have aspired. And when that tooth—I do not say fang, for it came from no lion or serpent or grotesque antediluvian beast, but was in form a *man's* tooth, somehow monstrously magnified—began to bite into me, I should without fail have been sliced thinner than a sausage at a lunch counter.

Closer and closer, over what seemed hours, descended the pendulum and that supernally terrifying instrument of destruction at which I could but gaze in dread, almost mesmerized fascination. Already I could feel the sinister wind of its passage with each swing. Soon, soon—Soon, how much more I would feel!

From far above, a soft but clear voice called, "Will you not return that which you have stolen?"

"Stolen?" I said, and my own voice held a new terror, for I pride myself, and with justice, on being an honest man. "I have stolen nothing—nothing, do you hear me?"

"I hear lies; naught save lies." The inquisitor, I thought, spoke more in sorrow than in anger. "Even now, that which you purloined remains with you to embellish your person and salve your vanity."

"Lies! You are the one who lies!" I cried, my desperation rising as the pendulum, the terrible pendulum, perceptibly descended.

"Having granted you the opportunity to repent of your crimes, I now give you the punishment you have earned both for your sin and for your failure of repentance," the inquisitor declared. "I wash my hands of you, Legrand, and may God have mercy upon your immortal soul."

Again the pendulum lowered, and lowered, and, Lord help me, lowered once more. Its next stroke sliced through some of the lashings binding me to that sacrificial platform. The one following that would surely slice through me. My eyes arced with the inexorable motion of the ball and its appended cutting tooth. I watched it reach the high point of its trajectory, and then, moaning with fear at was to come, I watched it commence its surely fatal descent. I screamed—

And I awoke with Helen beside me, warm in my own bed and altogether unbisected.

After these two most vivid dreams, I trust you will understand why from that time forward I feared and shunned slumber no less than a hydrophobic hound fights shy of water. The hound in due course expires of his distemper. Not being diseased in any normal sense, I did not perish, and the natural weakness of my mortal flesh did cause me occasionally to yield to the allurements of Morpheus despite my fear of what might come to pass if I did.

One night, asleep despite all wishes and efforts to remain awake, I fancied myself—indeed, in my mind, I *was*—guilty of some heinous crime. I had done it, and I had concealed it, concealed it so perfectly no human agency could have hoped to discover my guilt. Yes, officers of the police had come, but purely *pro forma*. That the crime had been committed at all was even, in their minds, a question; that I was in any way connected to it had never once occurred to them.

We sat down to confer together in the very chamber where the nefarious deed was done. I was, at first, charming and witty. But something then began to vex me, something at first so slight as to be all but imperceptible—certainly so to the minions of the law with whom I was engaged. And yet it grew and grew and grew within the confines of my mind to proportions Brobdingnagian. It was *a low, dull pain—much such a pain as a tooth makes when commencing to ache*. I gasped for breath— and yet the officers, lucky souls, felt it not.

I grew nervous, agitated, *distrait*, for the pounding in my mouth grew worse and worse. Soon I felt I must cry out or perish. It hurt more and more and more!—and at last, unable to suffer such anguish for another instant, I cried, "I admit the deed! Tear out the tooth!"—and I pointed to the one in question. "Here, here!—it is the paroxysm of this hideous bicuspid!"

Then, as before, I awoke in a house all quiet and serene; all quiet and serene but for me, I should say, for I lay with my heart audibly thudding as if in rhythm to the tintinnabulation of a great iron bell, my night-clothes drenched with the fetid perspiration brought on by terror. I slept no more until dawn, and not a wink for two days afterwards, either.

I had begun to steel myself towards a course of action I should have called mad in any other, yet one seemingly needful in my particular, circumstance. Yet still I hesitated, for divers reasons that appeared to me good, beginning with my unwillingness to undergo yet more pain and suffering and ending with my disinclination to credit the conclusion towards which these nocturnal phantasms were driving me—or, it could be, I should say, beginning with the latter and ending with the former. So many dreams pass through the mendacious gate of ivory, it is easiest to believe they all do.

Whilst equivocating—indeed, tergiversating, for I knew in my heart of hearts the right course, yet found not the courage to pursue it—I again found I could no longer hold eyelid apart from eyelid despite the heroic use of every stimulant known to man. I yawned; I tottered; I fell into bed, more in hope than in expectation of true rest; I slept.

And, once more, I dreamt. I had thought my previous nightmare the worst that could ever befall any poor mortal, of no matter how sinful a character. This proves only the limits of my previous power of imagination, not of the horror to which I might subject myself in slumber—or rather, as I had begun to suspect, the horror to which some increasingly unwelcome interloper and cuckoo's egg might subject me.

I seemed to awake, not from sleep, but from some illness so grave and severe, so nearly fatal, as to have all but suspended permanently my every vital faculty. And, upon awakening, I found myself not in the bed in which I had surely had consciousness slip away from me, but lying on rude, hard planks in darkness absolute.

It was not night. Oh, it may have been night, but it was not night that made the darkness. This I discovered on extending my hands upwards and encountering, less than a foot above my face, more boards, these as rude and hard as the others. Reaching out to either side, I found, God help me, more still. *I had been laid in the tomb alive!*

But one question beat upon my mind as I beat uselessly, futilely, upon the inner confines of the coffin housing what soon would become in truth my mortal remains unless I found some means of egress—would I go utterly mad ere perishing of asphyxiation, or would I take my last stifling breath still in full possession of the faculty of reason and aware to the end of my imminent extinction? The devil and the deep sea are as nothing beside it.

My screams rang deafeningly loud in the wooden enclosure so altogether likely to enclose me forever. Perhaps God was kind, and I did not have earth surrounding me on all sides, six feet above and how many thousands of miles below? Perhaps some merciful soul, hearing the cries of one in his last extremity, would hurry to his rescue as the Good Samaritan did in our Lord's parable so long ago. I did not believe it, but what had I to lose?

Only after some little time had elapsed did I note what I was screaming, and in so doing startled myself even in the midst of the unsurpassable horror of interment untimely. No such commonplace expostulation as *Help me!* or *In God's name, let me out!* passed my lips. No; what I shouted in that moment of terror inexpressible was, "I will give it back! So help me, I will give it back!"

A monstrous shaking commenced, as from the earthquake that ravaged New Madrid in the days of my green youth. Was I saved? Had I lain in the mortuary after all, and was some kindly soul tipping over the casket to facilitate my liberation? Was that light—sweet, blissful light—beating on my eyelids, or was it no more than madness commencing to derange my sense?

With a supreme effort of will, I opened my eyes. There above me, more sublimely beautiful than any angel's, appeared my sweet Helen's face, illumined by a candle bright and lovelier, altogether more welcoming, than the sun. "Are you well, Bill?" she inquired anxiously. "You gave some great, convulsive thrashes in your sleep."

"I will give it back!" I said, as I had when I lay entombed, even if only within the bounds of my own mind. Helen laughed, reckoning me—as any reasonable person might—still half swaddled in my slumbers. Yet never in all my days was I more sincere, more intent, more determined.

As soon as I thought there was any probability, no matter how remote, of bearding the illustrious Vankirk in his den, I hurried thither as fast as shank's mare would carry me. Finding him there—a commendation to his diligence, a trait of character frequently allied to skill—I was so rude as to seize him by the lapels, at the same time crying, "Take it out! Take from my jaw this ghastly, ghostly fragment, untimely ripped from the maxilla of a man who, even from beyond the grave, has made it all too plain he desires—no, requires—a reunion of his *disiuncta membra*."

"My dear Legrand!" quoth Vankirk. "You desire me to remove the bicuspid I successfully—indeed, all but miraculously—transplanted to your jaw? What madness do you speak, sir?"

"If miracle this be, never let me see another," I replied. "A miracle is said to be a happening for the good, but no good has come to me of this. On the contrary; never have I known such nightmares, which word you may construe either metaphorically or literally, as best suits you." I spent the next little while explaining all that had eventuated since that tooth's taking residence in my head, and finished, "This being so, I implore you to get it hence; get it hence forthwith. I have returned to you because of your knowledge of chloroform and skill with the anaesthetic drug, yet were you to tell me you needs must extract this accursed bicuspid with no such alleviating anodyne, I should not hesitate in begging you to proceed."

"You are in earnest," Vankirk observed, and my answering nod, I dare say, closely approximated to that of a madman in its vehemence. He was for some time silent, examining me closely. "To eschew the use of chloroform in an extraction would show a beastly and barbarous cruelty to which no man aspiring to the merciful calling of dentistry should sink," he declared. "Come; seat yourself in my chair. I shall do as you wish, and charge not a penny for it; never let it be said I leave those seeking my services unsatisfied in any way."

I seized his hand. "God bless you," I said fervently, and of my own free will placed myself in the seat in whose counterparts I had undergone so many exquisite excruciations. As he took the bottle of liquid Lethe from its repository, I held up one finger. "A moment, if you please."

"Yes? What do you require now?"

"Have you any notion, any true notion, of the provenance of

this tooth? The more precisely you can return it, once drawn, to its former and even now rightful owner, the better, I think, for everyone."

"I know from whom I bought it," Vankirk answered, "and have a good notion of the haunts she frequents. I can, I believe, make nearly certain to deliver it to the proper cemetery—or, I should say, paupers' graveyard. Will that suffice you?"

Although staggered at the notion that the person who took the tooth which had so tormented me fro the reeking jaw of some dull-eyed, swollen corpse could possibly belong to the fair sex, I nodded once more. "You must do that very thing," I said. "You must swear by whatever you hold most dear and holy that you *will* do it; else I cannot answer for the consequences, either to you or to myself."

"By my mother's grave, Mr. Legrand—a fitting oath here, in my opinion—I shall do what you require of me," Vankirk said. The solemnity with which he spoke not failing to impress me, I lowered my head in agreement, as Jove is said to have done in days of yore. He commenced to removed the stopper from the jar of chloroform, but then, arresting the motion, sent my way a glance instinct with curiosity. "I trust I do infer correctly that you would have me extract the offending bicuspid—the suppositiously offending bicuspid—without attempting to implant in your maxilla another intended to replace it?"

"Not for all the gold in California, not for all the cotton in Alabama, not for all the swindlers in New York City would I ever again have some other man's dental apparatus rooted in my own jaw. This being so, yes, sir, your inference is accurate."

"Very well. You must be aware, your bite will suffer."

"Worse things than my bite will suffer should you disregard my wishes here. Go on, man; go on."

Bowing courteously, he said, "I obey," and did at last expose to the open air the contents of that small yet potent bottle. Once more he steeped a scrap of cloth in the oily liquid contained therein; to my nostrils came the heavy, sweetish odor of this incomparable product of human sagacity and ingenuity, this even before he pressed the cloth to my face and brought with it—oblivion.

When I woke up, my mouth was full of blood. Vankirk held up a basin for me to spit in. I did. Soon as I could talk straight, I asks him, "Is the blamed thing out of there?"

"It sure is," Vankirk says. He held up his pelican to prove it. I couldn't swear that was the same tooth. But it was all over blood and there was a hole in my mouth in the right place, so I expect it was. He goes on, "I will tell you something downright peculiar, Mr. Legrand. Is your head clear enough to follow me?"

"I will follow you wherever you may go," says I. "You may count on it. Tell me this downright peculiar thing."

"I have had to take out a good many transplanted teeth," Vankirk says. "They most often fail. You know this yourself." I nodded, on account of I know it much too well. He goes on, "They are not in the habit of taking root. By the nature of things, they cannot be. They are dead. That means they come out easy as you please. But not this one here."

"Is that a fact? Somehow, Mr. Vankirk, I am not much surprised."

"By what you have told me, I can see how you would not be. This tooth here hung on with both hands and both feet, you might say. It made itself a part of you, and did not want to leave. I have never seen that before in a transplanted tooth. I never expect to see it again. I feared I would harm your jawbone getting it out. It was clinging that tight—it truly was. But it is gone now," he says.

"A good thing, too," says I. "I will not miss it a bit, and you can bet on that. Now—are you sure you got it all?"

He held up the pelican again. There was the tooth. It looked pretty much like a whole tooth, I will tell you that. Vankirk, now, he took another look at it. He frowned a little. Says he, "I suppose it is just barely possible some tiny little piece of root may have got left behind. I do not think so, but it is just barely possible. If it troubles you after this wound heals up, you come back, and I will go in there after it."

"I will do that very thing. You may rely on it," says I.

But that was a while ago now, and my teeth have not given me any trouble since. Well, that is not true. I have had some of the usual sort. I have the measure of that, though. With this new chloroform, I hardly even fear going to the tooth-drawer. I have not had any trouble of the other kind. I have not had any dreams of the sort I had with that tooth in my head. Those dreams would stagger an opium-eater, and that is nothing but the truth.

They are gone now. Thank heavens for that. Vankirk is a smart fellow, but this time he outsmarted himself. He did yank every bit of that miserable tooth, and he fooled himself when he thought he might not have. I am glad he fooled himself, too, which is one more thing you may take to the bank.

In fact, George M., I am so glad that dreadful tooth is truly gone and will trouble me no more, I am going to ask you to set things up again for everybody, so my friends here can help me celebrate.

Amontillado, all around!

REINCARNATION

I sold this one to *Amazing*'s Pat Price at the party following the Nebula banquet in Los Angeles in 1988. Anything else I say about it would be longer than the story, so I won't.

"IT'S TRUE!" HARRISON SMEDLEY CRIED, LOOKING UP AT last from the tomes over which he had pored for years. "Reincarnation is true, and I shall prove it!"

Before his wife could stop him, he walked off the balcony of their fifteenth-floor apartment and plunged smiling to his death.

He was right. The very next day, someone bought him and wore him for a boutonniere.

THE PHANTOM TOLBUKHIN

This is an alternate history involving the aftermath of a German victory in World War II. Fedor Tolbukhin was a prominent Soviet general during the war. His name, coupled with the epithet I used, also suggests a famous children's book and lets me indulge a low taste for puns I'm sure you've never, ever noticed before.

GENERAL FEDOR TOLBUKHIN TURNED TO HIS POLITICAL commissar. "Is everything in your area of responsibility in readiness for the assault, Nikita Sergeyevich?"

"Fedor Ivanovich, it is," Nikita Khrushchev replied. "There can be no doubt that the Fourth Ukrainian Front will win another smashing victory against the fascist lice who suck the blood from the motherland."

Tolbukhin's mouth tightened. Khrushchev should have addressed him as *Comrade General*, not by his first name and patronymic. Political commissars had a way of thinking they were as important as real soldiers. But Khrushchev, unlike some—unlike most—political commissars Tolbukhin knew, was not afraid to get gun oil on his hands, or even to take a PPSh41 submachine gun up to the front line and personally pot a few fascists.

"Will you inspect the troops before ordering them to the assault against Zaporozhye?" Khrushchev asked.

"I will, and gladly," Tolbukhin replied.

Not all of Tolbukhin's forces were drawn up for inspection, of course: too great a danger of marauding *Luftwaffe* fighters spotting such an assemblage and shooting it up. But representatives from each of the units the Soviet general had welded into a solid fighting force were there, lined up behind the red banners that symbolized their proud records. Yes, they were all there: the flags of the First Guards Army, the Second

Guards, the Eighth Guards, the Fifth Shock Army, the Thirty-eighth Army, and the Fifty-first.

"Comrade Standard Bearer!" Tolbukhin said to the young soldier who carried the flag of the Eighth Guards Army, which bore the images of Marx and Lenin and Stalin.

"I serve the Soviet Union, Comrade General!" the standard bearer barked. But for his lips, he was utterly motionless. By his wide Slavic face, he might have come from anywhere in the USSR; his mouth proved him a native Ukrainian, for he turned the Great Russian *G* into an *H*.

"We all serve the Soviet Union," Tolbukhin said. "How may we best serve the motherland?"

"By expelling from her soil the German invaders," the young soldier replied. "Only then can we take back what is ours. Only then can we begin to build true Communism. It surely will come in my lifetime."

"It surely will," Tolbukhin said. He nodded to Khrushchev, who marched one pace to his left, one pace to the rear. "If all the men are as well indoctrinated as this one, the Fourth Ukrainian Front cannot fail."

After inspecting the detachments, he conferred with the army commanders—and, inevitably, with their political commissars. They crowded a tumbledown barn to overflowing. By the light of a kerosene lantern, Tolbukhin bent over the map, pointing out the avenues of approach the forces would use. Lieutenant General Yuri Kuznetsov, commander of the Eighth Guards Army, grinned wide enough to show a couple of missing teeth. "It is a good plan, Comrade General," he said. "The invaders will regret ever setting foot in the Soviet Union."

"I thank you, Yuri Nikolaievich," Tolbukhin said. "Your knowledge of the approach roads to the city will help the attack succeed."

"The fascist invaders *already* regret ever setting foot in the Soviet Union," Khrushchev said loudly.

Lieutenant General Kuznetsov dipped his head, accepting the rebuke. "I serve the Soviet Union!" he said, as if he were a raw recruit rather than a veteran of years of struggle against the Hitlerites.

"You have the proper Soviet spirit," Tolbukhin said, and even the lanternlight was enough to show how Kuznetsov flushed with pleasure.

Lieutenant General Ivanov of the First Guards Army turned to Major General Rudzikovich, who had recently assumed command of the Fifth Shock Army, and murmured, "Sure as the devil's grandmother, the Phantom will make the Nazis pay."

Tolbukhin didn't think he was supposed to hear. But he was young for his rank—only fifty-three—and his ears were keen. The nickname warmed him. He'd earned it earlier in the war—the seemingly endless war—against the madmen and ruffians and murderers who followed the swastika. He'd always had a knack for hitting the enemies of the peasants and workers of the Soviet Union where they least expected it, then fading away before they could strike back at his forces.

"Has anyone any questions about the plan before we continue the war for the liberation of Zaporozhye and all the territory of the Soviet Union now groaning under the oppressor's heel?" he asked.

He thought no one would answer, but Rudzikovich spoke up: "Comrade General, are we truly wise to attack the city from the northeast and southeast at the same time? Would we not be better off concentrating our forces for a single strong blow?"

"This is the plan the council of the Fourth Ukrainian Front has made, and this is the plan we shall follow," Khrushchev said angrily.

"Gently, gently," Tolbukhin told his political commissar. He turned back to Rudzikovich. "When we hit the Germans straight on, that is where we run into trouble. Is it not so, Anatoly Pavlovich? We will surprise them instead, and see how they like that."

"I hope it won't be too expensive, that's all," Major General Rudzikovich said. "We have to watch that we spend our brave Soviet soldiers with care these days."

"I know," Tolbukhin answered. "Sooner or later, though, the Nazis have to run out of men." Soviet strategists had been saying that ever since the Germans, callously disregarding the treaty Ribbentrop had signed with Foreign Commissar Molotov, invaded the USSR. General Tolbukhin pointed to the evidence: "See how many Hungarian and Romanian and Italian soldiers they have here in the Ukraine to pad out their own forces."

"And they cannot even station the Hungarians and Romanians next to one another, lest they fight," Khrushchev added—like any political commissar, if he couldn't score points off Rudzikovich one way, he'd try another. "Thieves fall out. It is only one more proof that the dialectic assures our victory. So long as we labor like Stakhanovites, over and above the norm, that victory will be ours."

"Anatoly Pavlovich, we have been over the plan a great many times," Tolbukhin said, almost pleadingly. "If you seek to alter it now, just before the attack goes in, you will need a better reason than 'I hope.' "

Anatoly Rudzikovich shrugged. "I hope you are right, Comrade General," he said, bearing down heavily on the start of the sentence. He shrugged again. "Well, *nichevo*." *It can't be helped* was a Russian foundation old as time.

Tolbukhin said, "Collect your detachments, Comrades, and rejoin your main forces. The attack *will* go in on time. And we shall strike the fascists a heavy blow at Zaporozhye. For Stalin and the motherland!"

"For Stalin and the motherland!" his lieutenants chorused. They left the barn with their political commissars—all but Lieutenant General Yuri Kuznetsov, whose Eighth Guards Army was based at Collective Farm 122 nearby.

"This attack *must* succeed, Fedor Ivanovich," Khrushchev said quietly. "The situation in the Ukraine requires it."

"I understand that, Nikita Sergeyevich," Tolbukhin answered, as quietly. "To make sure the attack succeeds, I intend to go in with the leading wave of troops. Will you fight at my side?"

In the dim light, he watched Khrushchev. Most political commissars would have looked for the nearest bed under which to hide at a request like that. Khrushchev only nodded. "Of course I will."

"Stout fellow." Tolbukhin slapped him on the back. He gathered up Kuznetsov and his political commissar by eye. "Let's go."

The night was very black. The moon, nearly new, would not rise till just before sunup. Only starlight shone down on Tolbukhin and his comrades. He nodded to himself. The armies grouped together into the Fourth Ukrainian Front would be all the harder for German planes to spot before they struck Zaporozhye. Dispersing them would help there, too.

He wished for air cover, then shrugged. He'd wished for a great many things in life he'd ended up not receiving. He remained alive to do more wishing. *One day*, he thought, *and one day soon, may we see more airplanes blazoned with the red star.* He was too well indoctrinated a Marxist-Leninist to recognize that as a prayer.

Waiting outside Collective Farm 122 stood the men of the Eighth Guards Army. Lieutenant General Kuznetsov spoke to them: "General Tolbukhin not only sends us into battle against the Hitlerite oppressors and bandits, he leads us into battle against them. Let us cheer the Comrade General!"

"*Urra!*" The cheer burst from the soldiers' throats, but softly, cautiously. Most of the men were veterans of many fights against the Nazis. They knew better than to give themselves away too soon.

However soft those cheers, they heartened Tolbukhin. "We shall win tonight," he said, as if no other alternative were even imaginable. "We shall win for Comrade Stalin, we shall win for the memory of the great Lenin, we shall win for the motherland."

"We serve the Soviet Union!" the soldiers chorused. Beside Tolbukhin, Khrushchev's broad peasant face showed a broad peasant grin. These were indeed well-indoctrinated men.

They were also devilishly good fighters. To Tolbukhin's mind, that counted for more. He spoke one word: "*Vryed'!*" Obedient to his order, the soldiers of the Eighth Guards Army trotted forward.

Tolbukhin trotted along with them. So did Khrushchev. Both the general and the political commissar were older and rounder than the soldiers they commanded. They would not have lost much face had they failed to keep up. Tolbukhin intended to lose no face whatever. His heart pounded. His lungs burned. His legs began to ache. He kept on nonetheless. So did Khrushchev, grimly slogging along beside him.

He expected the first brush with the *Wehrmacht* to take place outside of Zaporozhye, and so it did. The Germans patrolled east of the city: no denying they were technically competent soldiers. Tolbukhin wished they were less able; that would have spared the USSR endless grief.

A voice came out of the night: "*Wer geht hier?*" A hail of rifle and submachine-gun bullets answered that German hail. Tolbukhin hoped his men wiped out the patrol before the Nazis could use their wireless set. When the Germans stopped shooting back, which took only moments, the Eighth Guards Army rolled on.

Less than ten minutes later, planes rolled out of the west. Along with the soldiers in the first ranks, Tolbukhin threw himself flat. He ground his teeth and cursed under his breath. Had that patrol got a signal out after all? He hoped it was not so. Had prayer been part of his ideology, he would have prayed it was not so. If the Germans learned of the assault too soon, they could blunt it with artillery and rockets at minimal cost to themselves.

The planes—Tolbukhin recognized the silhouettes of Focke-Wulf 190s—zoomed away. They dropped neither bombs nor flares, and did not strafe the men of the Fourth Ukrainian Front. Tolbukhin scrambled to his feet. "Onward!" he called.

Onward the men went. Tolbukhin felt a glow of pride. After so much war, after so much heartbreak, they still retained their revolutionary spirit. "Truly, these are the New Soviet Men," he called to Khrushchev.

A middle-aged Soviet man, the political commissar nodded. "We shall never rest until we drive the last of the German invaders from our soil. As Comrade Stalin said, 'Not one step back!' Once the fascists are gone, we shall rebuild this land to our hearts' desire."

Tolbukhin's heart's desire was piles of dead Germans in field-gray uniforms, clouds of flies swarming over their stinking bodies. And he had achieved his heart's desire many times. But however many Nazis the men under his command killed, more kept coming out of the west. It hardly seemed fair.

Ahead loomed the apartment blocks and factories of Zaporozhye, black against the dark night sky. German patrols enforced their blackout by shooting into lighted windows. If they hit a Russian mother or a sleeping child . . . it bothered them not in the least. Maybe they won promotion for it.

"Kuznetsov," Tolbukhin called through the night.

"Yes, Comrade General?" the commander of the Eighth Guards Army asked.

"Lead the First and Second Divisions by way of Tregubenko Boulevard," Tolbukhin said. "I will take the Fifth and Ninth

Divisions farther south, by way of Metallurgov Street. Thus we will converge upon the objective."

"I serve the Soviet Union!" Kuznetsov said.

Zaporozhye had already been fought over a good many times. As Tolbukhin got into the outskirts of the Ukrainian city, he saw the gaps bombs and shellfire had torn in the buildings. People still lived in those battered blocks of flats and still labored in those factories under German guns.

In the doorway to one of those apartment blocks, a tall, thin man in the field-gray tunic and trousers of the *Wehrmacht* was kissing and feeling up a blond woman whose overalls said she was a factory worker. *A factory worker supplementing her income as a Nazi whore*, Tolbukhin thought coldly.

At the sound of booted feet running on Metallurgov Street, the German soldier broke away from the Ukrainian woman. He shouted something. Submachine-gun fire from the advancing Soviet troops cut him down. The woman fell, too, fell and fell screaming. Khrushchev stopped beside her and shot her in the back of the neck. The screams cut off.

"Well done, Nikita Sergeyevich," Tolbukhin said.

"I've given plenty of traitors what they deserve," Khrushchev answered. "I know how. And it's always a pleasure."

"Yes," Tolbukhin said: of course a commissar would see a traitor where he saw a whore. "We'll have to move faster now, though; the racket will draw the fascists. *Nichevo*. We'd have bumped into another Nazi patrol in a minute or two, anyway."

One thing the racket did not do was bring people out of their flats to join the Eighth Guards Army in the fight against the fascist occupiers. As the soldiers ran, they shouted, "Citizens of Zaporozhye, the hour of liberation is at hand!" But the city had seen a lot of war. Civilians left here were no doubt cowering under their beds, hoping no stray bullets from either Soviet or German guns would find them.

"Scouts forward!" Tolbukhin shouted as his men turned south from Metallurgov onto Pravdy Street. They were getting close to their objective. The fascists surely had guards in the area—but where? Finding them before they set eyes on the men of the Eighth Guards Army could make the difference between triumph and disaster.

Then the hammering of gunfire broke out to the south. Khrushchev laughed out loud. "The Nazis will think they are engaging the whole of our force, Fedor Ivanovich," he said joyfully. "For who would think even the Phantom dared divide his men so?"

Tolbukhin ran on behind the scouts. The Nazis were indeed pulling soldiers to the south to fight the fire there, and didn't discover they were between two fires till the Eighth Guards Army and, moments later, the men of the Fifth Shock Army and the Fifty-first Army opened up on them as well. How the Hitlerites howled!

Ahead of him, a German machine gun snarled death—till grenades put the men handling it out of action. Then, a moment later, it started up again, this time with Red Army soldiers feeding it and handling the trigger. Tolbukhin whooped with glee. An MG-42 was a powerful weapon. Turning it on its makers carried the sweetness of poetic justice.

One of his soldiers pointed and shouted: "The objective! The armory! And look, Comrade General! Some of our men are already inside. We have succeeded."

"We have not succeeded yet," Tolbukhin answered. "We will have succeeded only when we have done what he came here to do." He raised his voice to a great shout: "Form a perimeter around the building. Exploitation teams, forward! You know your assignments."

"Remember, soldiers of the Soviet Union, the motherland depends on your courage and discipline," Khrushchev added.

As Tolbukhin had planned, the perimeter force around the Nazi armory was as small as possible; the exploitation force, made up of teams from each army of the Fourth Ukrainian Front, as large. Tolbukhin went into the armory with the exploitation force. Its mission here was far the most important for the strike against Zaporozhye.

Inside the armory, German efficiency came to the aid of the Soviet Union. The Nazis had arranged weapons and ammunition so their own troops could lay hold of whatever they needed as quickly as possible. The men of the Red Army happily seized rifles and submachine guns and the ammunition that went with each. They also laid hands on a couple of more MG-42s. If they could get those out of the city, the fascists would regret it whenever they tried driving down a road for a hundred kilometers around.

"When you're loaded up, get out!" Tolbukhin shouted. "Pretty soon, the Nazis will hit us with everything they've got." He did not disdain slinging a German rifle on his back and loading his pockets with clips of ammunition.

"We have routed them, Fedor Ivanovich," Khrushchev said.

When Tolbukhin did not reply, the political commissar added, "A million rubles for your thoughts, Comrade General."

Before the war, the equivalent sum would have been a kopeck. Of course, before the war Tolbukhin would not have called the understrength regiment he led a front. Companies would not have been styled armies, nor sections divisions. "Inflation is everywhere," he murmured, and then spoke to Khrushchev: "As long as you came in, Nikita Sergeyevich, load up, and then we'll break away if we can, if the Germans let us."

Khrushchev affected an injured look. "Am I then only a beast of burden, Fedor Ivanovich?"

"We are all only beasts of burden in the building of true Communism," Tolbukhin replied, relishing the chance to get off one of those sententious bromides at the political commissar's expense. He went on, "I am not too proud to load myself like a beast of burden. Why should you be?"

Khrushchev flushed and glared furiously. In earlier days—in happier days, though Tolbukhin would not have thought so at the time—upbraiding a political commissar would sure have caused a denunciation to go winging its way up through the Party hierarchy, perhaps all the way up to Stalin himself. So many good men had disappeared in the purges that turned the USSR upside down and inside out between 1936 and 1938: Tukhashevsky and Koniev, Yegorov and Blyukher, Zhukov and Uborevich, Gamarnik and Fedko. Was it any wonder the Red Army had fallen to pieces when the Nazis attacked in May 1941?

And now, in 1947, Khrushchev was as high-ranking a political commissar as remained among the living. To whom could he denounce Tolbukhin? No one, and he knew it. However furious he was, he started filling his pockets with magazines of Mauser and Schmeisser rounds.

Sometimes, Tolbukhin wondered why he persisted in the fight against the fascists when the system he served, even in its tattered remnants, was so onerous. The answer was not hard to find. For one thing, he understood the difference between bad and worse. And, for another, he'd been of general's rank when the Hitlerites invaded the motherland. If they caught him, they would liquidate him—their methods in the Soviet Union made even Stalin's seem mild by comparison. If he kept fighting, he might possibly—just possibly—succeed.

Khrushchev clanked when turning back to him. The tubby little political commissar was still glaring. "I am ready, Fedor Ivanovich," he said. "I hope you are satisfied."

"*Da*," Tolbukhin said. He hadn't been satisfied since Moscow and Leningrad fell, but Khrushchev couldn't do anything about that. Tolbukhin pulled from his pocket an officer's whistle and blew a long, furious blast. "Soldiers of the Red Army, we have achieved our objective!" he shouted in a great voice. "Now we complete the mission by making our departure!"

He was none too soon. Outside, the fascists were striking heavy blows against his perimeter teams. But the fresh men coming out of the armory gave the Soviets new strength and let them blast open a corridor to the east and escape.

Now it was every section—every division, in the grandiose language of what passed for the Red Army in the southern Ukraine these days—for itself. Inevitably, men fell as the units made their way out of Zaporozhye and onto the steppe. Tolbukhin's heart sobbed within him each time he saw a Soviet soldier go down. Recruits were so hard to come by these days. The booty he'd gained from this raid would help there, and would also help bring some of the bandit bands prowling the steppe under the operational control of the Red Army. With more men, with more guns, he'd be able to hurt the Nazis more the next time.

But if, before he got out of Zaporozhye, he lost all the men he had now . . . *What then, Comrade General?* he jeered at himself.

Bullets cracked around him, spattering off concrete and striking blue sparks when they ricocheted from metal. He lacked the time to be afraid. He had to keep moving, keep shouting orders, keep turning back and sending another burst of submachine-gun fire at the pursuing Hitlerites.

Then his booted feet thudded on dirt, not on asphalt or concrete any more. "Out of the city!" he cried exultantly.

And there, not far away, Khrushchev doggedly pounded along. He had grit, did the political commissar. "Scatter!" he called to the men within the sound of his voice. "Scatter and hide your booty in the secure places. Resume the *maskirovka* that keeps us all alive."

Without camouflage, the Red Army would long since have become extinct in this part of the USSR. As things were, Tolbukhin's raiders swam like fish through the water of the Soviet peasantry, as Mao's Red Chinese did in their long guerrilla struggle against the imperialists of Japan.

But Tolbukhin had little time to think about Mao, either, for the Germans were going fishing. Nazis on foot, Nazis in armored cars and personnel carriers, and even a couple of panzers came forth from Zaporozhye. At night, Tolbukhin feared the German foot soldiers more than the men in machines. Machines were easy to elude in the darkness. The infantry would be the ones who knew what they were doing.

Still, this was not the first raid Tolbukhin had led against the Germans, nor the tenth, nor the fiftieth, either. What he did not know about rear guards and ambushes wasn't worth knowing. His men stung the Germans again and again, stung them and then crept away. They understood the art of making many men seem few, few seem many. Little by little, they shook off pursuit.

Tolbukhin scrambled down into a *balka* with Khrushchev and half a dozen men from the Eighth Guards Army, then struggled up the other side of the dry wash. They started back toward Collective Farm 122, where, when they were not raiding, they labored for their Nazi masters as they had formerly labored for their Soviet masters.

"Wait," Tolbukhin called to them, his voice low but urgent. "I think we still have Germans on our tail. This is the best place I can think of to make them regret it."

"We serve the Soviet Union!" one of the soldiers said. They returned and took cover behind bushes and stones. So did Tolbukhin. He could not have told anyone how or why he believed the fascists remained in pursuit of this little band, but he did. *Instinct of the hunted*, he thought.

And the instinct did not fail him. Inside a quarter of an hour, men in coal-scuttle helmets began going down into the *balka*. One of them tripped, stumbled, and fell with a thud. "Those God-damned stinking Russian pigdogs," he growled in guttural German. "They'll pay for this. Screw me out of sack time, will they?"

"*Ja*, better we should screw their women than they should screw us out of sack time," another trooper said. "That Natasha in the soldiers' brothel, she's limber like she doesn't have any bones at all."

"Heinrich, Klaus, *shut up!*" another voice hissed. "You've got to play the game like those Red bastards are waiting for us on the far side of this miserable gully. You don't, your family gets a *Fallen for Führer and Fatherland* telegram one fine day." By the way the other two men fell silent, Tolbukhin concluded that fellow was a corporal or sergeant. From his hiding place, he kept an eye on the sensible Nazi. *I'll shoot you first*, he thought.

Grunting and cursing—but cursing in whispers now—the Germans started making their way up the side of the *balka*. Yes, there was the one who kept his mind on business. Kill enough of that kind and the rest grew less efficient. The Germans got rid of Soviet officers and commissars on the same brutal logic.

Closer, closer . . . A submachine gun spat a great number of bullets, but was hardly a weapon of finesse or accuracy. "Fire!" Tolbukhin shouted, and blazed away. The Nazi noncom tumbled down the steep side of the wash. Some of those bullets had surely bitten him. The rest of the German squad lasted only moments longer. One of the Hitlerites lay groaning till a Red Army man went down and cut his throat. Who could guess how long he might last otherwise? Too long, maybe.

"*Now* we go on home," Tolbukhin said.

They had practiced withdrawal from such raids many times before, and *maskirovka* came naturally to Soviet soldiers. They took an indirect route back to the collective farm, concealing their tracks as best they could. The Hitlerites sometimes hunted them with dogs. They knew how to deal with that, too. Whenever they came to rivulets running through the steppe, they trampled along in them for a couple of hundred meters, now going one way, now the other. A couple of them also had their canteens filled with fiery pepper-flavored vodka. They poured some on their trail every now and then; it drove the hounds frantic.

"Waste of good vodka," one of the soldiers grumbled.

"If it keeps us alive, it isn't wasted," Tolbukhin said. "If it keeps us alive, we can always get outside of more later."

"The Comrade General is right," Khrushchev said. Where he was often too familiar with Tolbukhin, he was too formal with the men.

This time, though, it turned out not to matter. One of the other soldiers gave the fellow who'd complained a shot in the ribs with his elbow. "*Da*, Volya, the Phantom is right," he said. "The Phantom's been right a lot of times, and he hasn't hardly been wrong yet. Let's give a cheer for the Phantom."

It was another soft cheer, because they weren't quite safe yet, but a cheer nonetheless: "*Urra* for the Phantom Tolbukhin!"

Maybe, Tolbukhin thought as a grin stretched itself across his face, *maybe we'll lick the Hitlerites yet, in spite of everything.* He didn't know whether he believed that or not. He knew he'd keep trying. He trotted on. Collective Farm 122 wasn't far now.

MOSO

"Moso" is also an alternate history, but of a different sort—an ecological a-h, you might say. Each member of the cat family chooses prey based not least on size. Cats eat mice; bobcats eat ground squirrels; and so on up to leopards, which eat things like baboons and smaller antelopes, and lions, which eat larger antelopes and zebras. No feline big enough to hunt critters like rhinos and elephants ever evolved. But what if one did?

TSHINGANA SAW THE VULTURES SPIRALING DOWN FROM THE sky as he walked out from the kraal to the cattle. Many, many vultures were descending. Something large must have died, Tshingana thought, and not far away. He trotted through the scrubby grass to see what it was.

Large indeed: an elephant lay not far from a stand of acacia trees. The vultures hopped around, not getting too close to the great mountain of meat. Other, larger scavengers were there before them—hunting dogs; hyenas; and three lions, one a big, black-maned male. Tshingana's hand tightened round the knobkerrie he was carrying, through he was nearly a quarter-mile away, not close enough to be interesting.

Not even the lion showed any inclination to approach the elephant's carcass. Tshingana understood why a moment later, when a moso climbed up onto its prey and began to feed.

The youth dropped his club. He shivered all over, though the morning was already warm. He had never seen a moso before. Now he understood why the storytellers of the baTlokwa tribe likened the greatest of all cats to lightning and fire. What but lightning, fire, or a moso could bring down an elephant?

The moso would have made three, perhaps four, of the big male lion. Even across several hundred yards, Tshingana could see its fangs gleaming as it tore chunk after chunk of flesh from the flank of the animal it had killed. Had it not been atop the elephant, though, he might never have spied it at all, for its striped coat, dark brown on tawny, was made for blending into grassland.

It raised its enormous head and looked toward Tshingana. Those golden eyes seemed to pierce his very soul. He shook his head, rejecting the idea. Surely he was too small and puny for the moso to notice.

So it seemed, for the beast started eating again. Tshingana remembered the cattle he was supposed to be tending. The rest of the boys in his *iNtanga*—his age group—would be angry at him for giving them more to do. He loped away with a ground-eating stride he could keep up for a couple of hours at a stretch.

The cattle were not that far away. The other herdboys jeered and waved their fists at Tshingana as he approached. "Was the inside of your hut too dark to remind you it's daytime?" asked the tallest of them, a skinny youth named Inyangesa.

"More likely he stopped for *ukuHlobonga* with one of the girls," suggested Tshingana's half-brother Sigwebana. Everyone laughed at that; Tshingana felt his face grow hot. Men and women did *ukuHlobonga* when they did not want to start children. None of the herdboys had yet spent seed even at night, though, so Sigwebana was just being rude. He was good at that, Tshingana thought.

"Where *were* you, Tshingana?" asked his best friend Mafunzi.

"I saw the vultures come down, so I went to see why," he answered.

"I didn't see that," Sigwebana said.

"*I* did," Mafunzi said, "and over from the east, the direction Tshingana came from. What was it, Tshingana?"

"A moso killed an elephant, over by the acacias. I saw it eating," Tshingana said importantly.

The rest of the youths stared at him, eyes wide and white in their black faces. Then Sigwebana snickered. "You lie, Tshingana," he said. "Come on, tell us who you were playing *ukuHlobonga* with. Was it Matiwane? She's pretty, isn't she?" His hips thrust obscenely.

Tshingana hit him. Yelling at each other, the two herdboys rolled in the dirt, punching and wrestling. The others cheered them on. Finally, with honors about even, they warily separated. Tshingana wiped dirt, dry grass, and a few bugs from his hide. "It's the truth," he told Sigwebana, who was doing the same thing. "Go look for yourself if you don't believe me. I hope the moso eats you, too."

"It wouldn't," Inyangesa said. "Moso don't bother with people, any more than lions with rabbits: not enough meat for them to worry about. Moso don't even bother much with cattle."

"How do you know so much about moso?" Mafunzi asked. "You've never seen one. Nobody in our *iNtanga* has ever seen one, or in the group older than we are, either. Nobody except Tshingana, I mean." He grinned at his friend.

"I don't think he saw one either," Inyangesa said.

Tshingana wanted to hit him too, but he'd just had one fight and was pretty sure Inyangesa could beat him. All he said was, "See for yourself. Take Sigwebana with you."

"We'll both come after you if you're lying," Inyangesa warned him. "By the acacias, you said?" He started trotting toward them. After a moment, Sigwebana followed.

"What will you do if they don't find it?" Mafunzi asked.

"So you don't really believe me either, do you?" Tshingana said bitterly. "It was there. They'll see it."

He and Mafunzi walked along, following the cattle and occasionally yelling and waving their arms to keep the beasts together. The herd was not a chief's fancy one, with all the cows the same color, but, Tshingana thought, that only mattered to chiefs—the milk was just as sweet either way.

Inyangesa and Sigwebana were gone so long, Tshingana began to worry. They might have been too small for the moso to care about, but more than a moso had been by the acacia trees. Some of the predators there were of a size to find herdboy a fine meal.

No, here they came, Tshingana saw with relief. Not even Sigwebana deserved to be eaten by hunting dogs . . . he supposed. Certainly it would set the kraal in an uproar if he was. On the other hand, if he was going to call Tshingana a liar—

He wasn't. He and Inyangesa were almost leaping out of their skins in excitement. "It's there! It's there!" they shouted, and Tshingana's heart leaped too. He'd almost begun to doubt himself. He glanced over at Mafunzi. His friend had the grace to hang his head.

"Big as a—big as a—" Sigwebana seemed stuck for a comparison. Tshingana did not blame him. Only rhinos, hippos, and elephants were bigger than that moso. Tshingana's half-brother went on, "A lion got too close to the elephant's carcass, and the moso roared at it. It sounded just like thunder, but even more frightening. You should have seen that lion scramble backwards."

Inyangesa said, "I know it's not noon yet, but I think we should bring the cattle back to the kraal early. No one will be angry at us when we tell what we found."

"We?" Tshingana yelled in outrage. "Before you did not believe me, and now you want to take credit?" He balled his fists. He still did not want to fight Inyangesa, but it did not look as though he'd have much choice.

Then Mafunzi said, "For finding a moso, there is enough credit to go around." Inyangesa nodded. After a moment, so did Tshingana. Mafunzi was right.

The herdboys got the cattle turned round, though the beasts were inclined to balk at having routine broken. They moved so slowly and resentfully that it *was* nearly noon by the time the beehive huts and thorn fence of the kraal drew near.

Still, they were early enough to be noticed. Several of the women out hoeing in the millet fields around the kraal yelled at Tshingana and his companions. The yells turned to curses whenever the cattle tried to nibble the crops or stepped on the young plants nearest the track.

The commotion the women raised made the kraal's men look up from what they were doing. "Too early to milk the beasts yet!" shouted Mafunzi's father Ndogeni.

"But we saw—" Mafunzi began.

Shamagwava the smith shouted him down, as grown men shout down youths all over the world: "I don't care what you saw. Go back out and see it again till the proper time." Shamagwava was father to Tshingana and Sigwebana, by different wives. He was as burly as his trade would suggest—not a man to argue with, not at any normal time.

This time was not normal. "Father, we saw a moso!" the two half-brothers yelled together. Sigwebana even smiled at Tshingana afterwards. After years of squabbling, they'd found something about which they could agree completely.

Dead silence for a moment, almost as unusual round the kraal as mention of the greatest cat. Then all the men were shouting at once, most of them in high excitement. But Shamagwava said, "If they're making this up to keep from working . . . " As smith, he worked more steadily than the rest of the baTlokwa men, and had exaggerated notions about the value of labor.

Even as Shamagwava complained, though, Ndogeni asked, "Where did you see it?" The boys quickly told him. He got down on hands and knees to crawl into his hut. When he came out, he was carrying several assegais—throwing-spears as tall as he was, each with a span-long iron point—and his oval cowhide shield. Several other men also armed themselves. "We will go look," Ndogeni declared. They trotted off toward the stand of acacias, which was hardly visible from the kraal.

"They can't be thinking of hunting the moso!" Tshingana exclaimed. The assegais seemed flimsy as reeds to him, when set against the bulk and power of the elephant he had seen.

Shamagwava came out to him, set a hard hand on his shoulder. "If there is a moso, they will not hunt it," he said. "Why should they? Moso rarely trouble men or cattle. But they will drive the scavengers from the body of the elephant, so they can bring back fresh meat for us."

Tshingana's mouth watered. It occurred to him that the men were scavengers of the moso too, no less than the vultures or hunting dogs. He did not care. Meat was meat. He had never tasted elephant before.

His father brought *amaSi* to him and Sigwebana. They ate the milk curds and waited for the men to return. Mafunzi and Inyangesa started milking some of the kraal's cattle, but only halfheartedly. Their heads went up at every sound—they were waiting, too.

The cattle, impatient to get back to the scrub for the afternoon's grazing, lowed and tossed their heads. The herdboys, though, did not want to take them out, and the few men left at the kraal did not insist. As much as anything, that showed Tshingana how remarkable the moso was.

The sun was heading down toward the western hills before the band of men finally reappeared. They moved slowly; as they drew closer, Tshingana saw that they were burdened with as much meat as they could carry. His stomach growled. He patted it, anticipating a feast.

The women working in the fields set down their hoes and digging-sticks and rushed out toward the returning men with glad cries: they saw the meat too. "Raise the fires high tonight!" Inyangesa shouted.

Shamagwava turned to him. "Since you had the idea, you can gather the wood." Inyangesa's long, mobile face fell. Tshingana laughed as he sadly shambled off to start dragging in branches and dry grass. That was a mistake. "You can help," his father said.

Sigwebana was doubly foolish, for he had seen the fate of his companion and his half-brother but laughed anyhow. That drew Shamagwava's attention to him. With three boys hauling fuel, soon the fires could have been made big enough to roast food for the whole baTlokwa *impi*—big enough to cook for a regiment, not just the folk of this kraal.

Ndogeni, bent almost double under the great chunk of elephant meat on his back, set down his load with a sigh of relief. Flies descended on it in a buzzing cloud. Ndogeni took no notice of them. He walked over to Tshingana and spoke to him most seriously, as if he were a man and a warrior: "There was a moso, Tshingana. We saw it just as it was leaving the carcass, and heard it too."

Inyangesa's father Uhamu, an even taller, thinner version of his son, shuddered as he lay down the meat he was carrying. "That roar is the deepest, most frightening sound I ever heard, a sound like the beginning of an earthquake. My bones turned to water; nothing could have made me draw close to it, even had I wished to."

Ndogeni nodded. "If you ask me, the moso is an *umThakathi*—a wizard—in the shape of a beast. It must be more than simply a big cat. A lion's roar is savage, but it does not put that heart-freezing dread in a man."

Uhamu visibly gathered himself. "It is gone now, though, and we have this lovely meat it left behind. And I will drink millet-beer, and after I have drunk enough I will forget I was ever frightened in all my life. And for that, the headache I will have tomorrow will be a small price to pay."

The elephant meat proved tough and strong-tasting. Tshingana ate his fill anyhow, as much for the novelty of it as for any other reason. He also drank a couple of pots of beer, which left him yawning even before the evening twilight was gone from the sky.

His mother Nandi was already snoring on her grass mat when he got down on all fours and crawled into the hut they shared. As soon as he closed the low door behind him, the hearthfire made the hut start to fill up with smoke. His eyes watered as he got his own sleeping-mat down from where it hung on the wall. He lay down.

The air was a little fresher near the ground, but smelled of the cow dung that had been pounded into the dirt to make a smooth floor. To Tshingana, it was part of the smell of home. Aided by the beer he'd drunk, he drifted toward sleep.

Cockroaches scuttled through the straw of the hut's walls, darted across the floor. One scurried over Tshingana's leg. He was snoring himself by then, and never noticed.

THE MOSO WANDERED AWAY FROM THE KRAAL, FOLLOWING the elephants on which it preyed. The brief notoriety that had accrued to Tshingana for first spying the beast slowly faded as newer matters caught the fancy of his clan.

Among those newer matters, to Tshingana's mortification, was his half-brother Sigwebana's coming of age. The two of them had been born about the same time; Tshingana had always assumed he would reach puberty first. But one night Sigwebana woke with his belly wet—manhood had come to him, while Tshingana remained a boy.

Sigwebana was revoltingly smug about the whole thing, too, which only made it worse. Tshingana vowed revenge, and got it. When a boy became a man among the baTlokwa, as among other nearby Bantu tribes, one morning he drove his kraal's cattle far out into the grassland, trying to hide them from everyone. The longer he succeeded, the greater the success expected from him in the future.

Tshingana stalked Sigwebana like a lion going after a gnu. It was not even noon when he found his half-brother and the cattle in a drift—a wash with a trickle of stream in the bottom—surprisingly close to the kraal.

He stood at the top of the drift, yelling and jeering, drawing boys and men to Sigwebana. Sigwebana wept and cursed and looked as though he wanted to throw his new man-sized assegai at Tshingana.

That evening, back at the kraal, his father took him aside. "You did well—maybe too well," Shamagwava said. "No one likes to be humiliated . . . and Sigwebana is my son too."

"He shouldn't have boasted so much," Tshingana said sullenly. He knew he ought to feel guilty, but could not manage it.

"I suppose not." Shamagwava sighed. "How do you imagine he will act, though, when your turn to hide the herd comes?"

Tshingana's lips skinned back from his teeth. "I hadn't thought about that," he said in a small voice.

"Maybe you should have," his father said. "Be sure Sigwebana will think of little else. I cannot even say I altogether blame him for it."

For the next few weeks, the problem of what Sigwebana would do remained only a worry at the back of Tshingana's mind. But then he awoke one night from a dream of confused but overwhelming sweetness, to discover that his seed had jetted forth for the first time. By the usages of the baTlokwa, he was a man.

He watched Sigwebana as he told Shamagwava he had spent himself in the night. His father pounded his back, almost knocking him down, and roared out the traditional bawdy congratulations. His half-brother, though, looked at him like a leopard studying an antelope from a thorn tree.

Shamagwava gave Tshingana a man's assegai, a weapon a foot taller than he was. "Tomorrow the cattle are yours, my son—for as long as you can keep them," he said. His eyes slipped to Sigwebana, who was, after all, also his son.

Knowing how his half-brother would go after him, Tshingana had no great hope of keeping the clan's herd undiscovered for very long. Staying on the loose till mid-afternoon would be fine. Anything better than Sigwebana had done would be fine.

Even if he thought he'd be quickly caught, Tshingana did not intend to make things easy for Sigwebana—or for the rest of the clan. He crawled out of his mother's hut just past midnight, a good deal earlier than it was customary for herdboys-turned-men to head off to hide the kraal's cattle.

The cattle were convinced it was too early. They lowed in sleepy protest as Tshingana moved aside the heavy poles that barred their pen. "Shut up!" he hissed. He knew Sigwebana would be up soon no matter what he did; he did not want the beasts rousing his half-brother all the earlier. That kept him from whacking them into motion with the shaft of the assegai, as he would have done otherwise. Instead, he gently coaxed them out of the pen and away.

Luckily the moon was only a couple of days past full. By its light Tshingana managed a fair pace, not what he could have done in daylight but much better than the crawl he would have had to use in real darkness.

As best he could and for as long as he could, he kept the herd to the same path it used going out to its usual grazing grounds. If fortune smiled, the tracks the cattle were making tonight would be hard to pick out from the thousands of other hoofprints, some fresh as yesterday, that pocked the grass.

The kraal was invisible by the time the eastern horizon lightened toward day. Tshingana danced a few steps—he'd come farther than he'd dared hope. In a while, he could start thinking about where to abandon the usual track and strike out for a proper hiding place.

Motion behind him, highlighted by the morning sun, made him whirl—was that, could that be, his pursuers already? Would he be laughed at for the rest of his life? But Tshingana's clansmen were not coming up; instead he saw a large herd of elephants ambling along, each immense beast now and then pausing to pull up a bush or clump of grass with its trunk and stuff the food into its mouth.

Where Tshingana had danced before, he sang now. If he could keep his herd headed in the direction the elephants were going, their huge feet would erase the tracks of the cattle. The men and boys from the kraal might never catch up to him! What sort of triumph would be foretold by his triumphant return home after they all gave up?

He shouted to the cattle, smacked a couple with his assegai. They had to move quickly now, to stay ahead of the elephants, and move in a tighter body than usual, too, so no stragglers' hoofprints would let his pursuers pick up the trail.

The cattle complained, but they were used to obeying herdboys. They would do what Tshingana wanted, at least for a while. The elephants were faster than they were, so eventually he would have to get out of the way. But not yet, he thought. Not yet.

Tshingana sang louder. Things were going better than he had ever dared hope. Even the elephants were cooperating, walking a fairly straight path that was easy to anticipate. They would hide the herd as a witch-doctor's mask hid his face while he was smelling out an *umThakathi*.

Just as Tshingana was starting to feel like a great chief (or as he imagined a great chief might feel), everything came apart at once. The elephants were about a quarter of a mile behind the cattle when Tshingana heard a low, rumbling roar that jabbed twin spears of ice into the small of his back.

The elephants' trunks went straight up into the air; their great fanlike ears stood away from their bodies. First one, then another, trumpeted the high shrill cry that meant danger.

The moso roared again. Tshingana partly heard that roar, partly felt it with some ancient part of his body that seemed specially made for knowing terror. He remembered what Uhamu and Ndogeni had said about the moso's roar. He had thought they were exaggerating. He thought so no longer. The moso's roar *made* him afraid, in the most bowel-loosening literal sense of the word.

The elephants were terrified too. They scattered in panic, running every which way. The ground shook under Tshingana's feet. The moso bounded after a cow elephant who fled with her ridiculous fly-whisk tail straight out behind her. With its bulk, the moso was not as fast as a lion, but it was faster than any elephant. Tshingana watched the great muscles ripple under its striped hide as it slammed into the cow.

Like a lion that had seized a gnu, the moso tried to drag the elephant off its feet. Its claw scored the cow's thick hide, leaving behind dripping lines of red. The elephant's screams grew even more frantic. The moso roared and bit, roared and bit.

Finally the moso pulled the elephant down. Tshingana heard the thud of that huge body slamming to the ground. Forgetting his own safety, he ran closer. He wanted to watch this greatest of all kills. Through the dust the other elephants had kicked up, through the cloud that surrounded the fallen female, it wasn't easy.

Even down, the female kept fighting, striking out with her big round feet at the moso, which clawed her belly like a wild cat ripping the guts out of a squirrel. Blood was everywhere now, on the elephant, on the ground, all over the moso. The moso was biting as well as clawing, trying to get a grip under the elephant's chin and throttle it.

Then, unexpectedly, the moso's roar rose to a shriek that made Tshingana stuff fingers in his ears. The cow elephant, still screaming itself, scrambled up onto its feet and lurched away. The moso slapped at it with a barbed foot as it escaped, took two or three shambling steps after it, and stopped. After a moment, Tshingana saw why: in the struggle, the elephant's bulk had crushed one of its hind legs.

The moso shrieked again, fury and torment mingled. Tshingana's flesh prickled. He was not used to feeling empathy for animals, but he did now, for the moso. A three-legged cat was as useless as a one-legged man—and no one would provide for the moso, as clansfolk might for a cripple.

However beasts know things, the moso must have known it was doomed. It sank back on its haunches, methodically licked the blood from its flanks and belly. It licked its ruined leg too, then let out a snort that said as clearly as words that it knew it would do no good.

But while the moso lived, it would try to keep on living. It snorted again, this time, Tshingana judged, in pain, as it got up. Only three legs touched the ground. Its enormous head swung back and forth, finally stopping, to his horror, on him. The moso growled, and that growl brought on the same freezing fear as its roar. It limped toward him—if it could not hunt elephants any more, smaller prey would have to do.

Tshingana fled. The moso came after him. For the first time, he wished his clansfolk had caught him hours ago. But he had done too good a job of hiding. He was on his own—he was a man. He wished—oh, how he wished!—he were a herdboy again.

He looked back over his shoulder at the moso, tripped over a root, and fell on his face. Thorns scratched his chest and arms. The shock and pain of the fall helped clear the panic from his head. His wits were working once more as he jumped up.

The moso still limped after him, remorseless as death. But Tshingana was faster now, and could change directions far more nimbly. If he kept his head, he was safe.

Safe, suddenly, was not enough. Instead of running, Tshingana danced toward to the moso. Its baleful yellow eyes followed him as it tried to turn to keep itself facing him. Had it roared, its fear would have made him run again. But it was silent, panting, watching to see what he would do.

He slipped round till it presented its left flank to him. There, he thought—just behind that stripe. That was where the assegai would have to go in. From ten or fifteen yards, he threw the spear. Then, weaponless, he fled in good earnest.

The moso screamed, a cry so loud and terrible he thought for a dreadful instant it was coming hard after him. But when he looked around, he saw it writhing on the ground, batting at the assegai with a forepaw. Each time it touched the shaft, it drove the point deeper into its side and screamed again.

Tshingana saw his cast, his first with a man's spear, had not been perfect. The assegai was sunk into a brown stripe, not the lighter fur in front of it for which he had aimed. The moso was making up for it, though; its frantic efforts to dislodge the spear simply stirred it through the beasts' vitals. At last it must have pierced the heart. The moso gave a convulsive shudder and lay still.

Tshingana looked around and gasped in dismay. The moso had made him commit the herder's ultimate sin—however briefly, he'd forgotten about his cattle. As cattle will, they had taken advantage of his inattention and were happily scattering themselves over the savannah.

He dashed after them, shouting and waving his arms. Rather grumpily, they acquiesced in being regathered into a tight knot—all but one, an old white cow with a crumpled horn that delighted in making herdboys' lives miserable.

After spearing a moso, Tshingana was not about to let a cow intimidate him. He screamed in its ears and threw clods of dirt at it. It lowed mournfully, baffled that its usual tactics were failing. Tshingana slapped it on the nose. Utterly defeated, it went back to the herd.

Tshingana cautiously went back to where the moso lay. Its eyes were glazed now; its flanks did not move. Blood ran from its mouth. Tshingana was sure it was dead . . . but not sure enough to risk getting in range of those dreadful claws. He picked up a long stick, prodded the end of the spearshaft with it.

Only when the great cat still did not move did Tshingana dare to reach for the assegai. Just as his fingers closed round it, he heard a shout, thin in the distance: "I see you, half-brother of mine, you worthless clump of cow dung!"

Tshingana's eyes flicked to the sun. It was into the western half of the sky. "I did better than you, Sigwebana," he yelled back.

His half-brother ran toward him. "You were just lucky, Tshingana," he said, still at the top of his lungs. "You didn't even really hide the cattle; I saw them from a long way away. All you did was a lot of running, so it took a while to catch up with you."

Tshingana glanced around. Sigwebana was right—the herd could have been much better hidden. Others had spotted it besides his half-brother, too; behind Sigwebana, Tshingana saw Inyangesa and his father Uhamu, and more clansfolk behind them.

Still . . . "How I did it doesn't matter, just that I did it," Tshingana said truthfully. "Besides, I've been busy with other things than hiding them prettily."

"Other things? Like what?" Sigwebana was getting close now, but not yet close enough to see through the thick, thigh-high grass in which Tshingana stood. "Like what?" he challenged again. "*UkuHlobonga*?"

"Go do *ukuHlobonga* between a hyena's thighs," Tshingana retorted. He jerked his assegai free, waved it to show Sigwebana the blood down half the length of the shaft. "I was busy with things like this."

"What did you spear, a rabbit?" Sigwebana pushed his way through the grass so he could find out what lay at Tshingana's feet. He looked at the dead moso, at his half-brother, at the moso again. "No," he whispered. "You didn't. You couldn't."

"Yes, I did," Tshingana said proudly. "Yes, I could."

"Did what, new man? Could what?" Uhamu came up, sweat making his lanky body gleam like polished ebony. As Sigwebana had, he stopped short when he saw the moso. "It wasn't dead when you found it?" he demanded sternly of Tshingana. Just behind Uhamu, Inyangesa stared at his friend.

"I speared it still alive," Tshingana declared.

Uhamu was studying the ground where the moso lay. "I believe you," he said at last. "I see how it twisted and fought when the assegai went home." He raised an eyebrow. "I suppose you also smashed its hind leg there."

Tshingana felt his face grow hot. "No, of course not." More and more men and boys from the kraal came up and listened while he told the story of how he had killed the moso.

"So that's why the elephants stampeded," Shamagwava said. He shook his head in wonder and put an arm round his son's shoulders. Tshingana felt nine feet tall. Shamagwava went on, "We were still a good ways behind you when that happened. I didn't think of the moso; I thought it had followed that other herd north."

"It must have doubled back," Tshingana agreed.

"So it must." Shamagwava shook his head again. "The first

moso near our kraal in years, and not only is it slain, but slain by my son, my son who has just become a man. How could a father be more proud?"

"You are lucky indeed, Shamagwava," Uhamu said. Mafunzi's father Ndogeni nodded. Mafunzi beamed at Tshingana, who smiled back at his friend. Inyangesa was smiling too, a little less certainly; he seemed to have trouble getting used to the idea that Tshingana was suddenly a person of consequence. Tshingana did not mind. He had trouble with that idea himself.

Sigwebana had not stayed around to listen to his half-brother praised. He was heading back toward the kraal, a small, lonely figure thinking in the distance. Tshingana had wanted to outdo him, yes, but he was not sure he'd wanted to outdo him like this. He might have made an enemy for life.

Tshingana supposed he would have to do something about that one day. Not today, though. Today his father was saying, "Now that you've killed the moso, my son, my man, have you thought about what you want to do next?"

"Two things, father." In the aftermath of the fight with the greatest cat, Tshingana found his mind clear as a stream in a pebbled bed. "For one, I want to make my warrior's shield from the moso's skin instead of cowhide, so everyone will know what I was able to do—and so I will never forget."

The clansmen murmured approvingly. Shamagwava said, "That is very fine, son. You will have a shield to make even an *inDuna*, a subchief, jealous. And what is the other thing?"

Tshigana grinned. "Now that I'm a man, I'm going to find out about *ukuHlobonga* for myself!"

BLUETHROATS

Have I ever gone birding around Nome with my daughter? Yes. Are the people in the story anything like her and me? No. And the lady I'm married to is just fine, for which I thank heaven every day. But Laura did see a golden-crowned sparrow in the back yard. She really did.

To get to where the bluethroats nest, you drive north out of Nome, up Bering Street. There's not much traffic, but you drive slowly and cautiously anyway. The pavement ends a few miles out of town, near the Dexter cutoff. The cutoff is dirt and gravel. So is the Kougarok road, the one that takes you to where the bluethroats may be.

"Pothole." Your daughter rides shotgun in the rental's passenger seat.

"I see it." And you drive around it. One jolt saved.

"When the roads are good, they're fine," your daughter says. "But when they're not . . . "

"They're not," you agree. They have signs on them: NO MAINTENANCE OCTOBER 1–MAY 1. It's June now. The sun shines twenty-two hours a day. It gets up into the fifties. The top few feet of the tundra thaw. Ponds and puddles and streams everywhere. Flowers blaze across the vastness. Millions of birds, which is why you're here. Billions of bugs, which is why the birds are.

Your daughter points to a scattering of houses ahead. "Must be Dexter."

"Uh-huh." Before you got here, you wouldn't have thought Nome, with not even 5,000 people, boasted suburbs. But you're driving through one. Houses. A lodge. A little sell-everything shop. Gone.

Nome is half small-town America, half really weird. Satellite

TV. Kids with backwards baseball caps and baggy jeans slouching around looking for something to do. An Italian-Japanese place run by Koreans—pretty good, actually.

But . . . A reindeer in a red collar in the back of an Eskimo's F-150. Musk oxen ambling around the slopes outside of town. More bars per capita than maybe anywhere. Loud, drunken arguments on the street outside your room at the Nugget Inn when the bars close at half past two.

It's about sunset then. Night, such as it is, barely gets dark enough for you to need headlights. Then, a little past four, the sun comes up again and you start over—if you ever stopped. Midnight softball—no lights—is a popular sport here. In the wintertime, so is ice golf on the frozen Bering Sea. And the Iditarod ends in Nome, across the street from the Nugget.

In the hotel lobby is a bigger-than-life photo of a bluethroat singing its head off. It's an Asian bird, but in summer it spills over and nests in western Alaska. It's sparrow-sized, but no other bird has that fancy blue-and-orange throat marking. If you want to see it in the States, you have to start from Nome.

A different photo of a bluethroat sits on the counter at the rental-car place, which operates out of the Aurora Inn, Nome's other hotel. A lot of the summer visitors here are birders, and the locals know it. Next to the photograph is a journal of what's been seen where. Nome is far, far away from the main highway system. But it sits at the center of its own network of 250 miles of these teeth-jarring roads. There's a hand-drawn map in the journal. A little past milepost 71 on the Kougarok road . . .

Plenty of birding to do on the way. A few miles up the road from Dexter, your daughter points to a roadside pool. "Shall we stop?"

"Sure." You pull over to the side. You're still half on the road, but so what? It's straight as a Republican senator. Anyone coming can see the car from a long way off. Not that anyone is. After Los Angeles, having a road to yourself seems stranger than anything else here.

You and your daughter get out. You spray each other with insect repellent and rub it on your cheeks and forehead. A few mosquitoes buzz lazily. Only a few: it's early yet, and cool, and you're not very far out onto the tundra. But Alaska mosquitoes are like nothing you've ever seen. Even a few are too many. A postcard on a rack at the Nugget Inn shows the business end of one silhouetted against a sunset, with the legend ALASKA'S STATE BIRD. Kidding, but kidding on the square.

Strapped binoculars thumping against your chests, the two of you walk over to the pool. Except for your footfalls and the wind in the dwarf willows, everything is quiet. Your ears don't know what to do with silence. Always something in L.A. An airplane overhead. Distant traffic. A neighbor's TV. Not loud, but always there.

Two brown shapes swimming in the pool. "Ducks?" your daughter says doubtfully.

You raise your binoculars. "Beavers!"

They don't give a damn about you. One swims to the edge of the pool, not twenty feet away. It's a female; it has teats. It strips off some willows branches and drags them into the water, not very far, to eat. It crunches as it chews. Who would have thought beavers were noisy eaters? Who would have thought you'd find out?

"Wow." Not much more than a whisper from your daughter. She goes on, a little louder, "I wish Mom could have seen this."

"Yeah." These past few days, you've walked out on the tundra. Most of it is springy and yielding underfoot. If you come down wrong, though, you fill your shoe with freezing water. You feel that way now. Two years ago, your wife lost what everybody called a brave battle against breast cancer. You don't argue. What point? You know how scared she was at the end, and in how much pain. Was that bravery? Perhaps it was. You go, "I—" and stop short.

One word too many. Your daughter sets her chin the way you do. "You were going to say something like, 'I wish Dave could have come along,' weren't you?"

"Well . . . " You don't deny it, but you don't admit it, either. One word!

"Cheating prick." Your daughter is going through a divorce. They both teach at the state university, Dave in linguistics, your daughter in anthropology. Dave is dating someone younger, someone blonder, someone altogether more tractable. Someone less like you, in other words.

You always liked him before the mess started. You still do, till you catch yourself and remember you shouldn't. Your daughter knows it. It pisses her off, bigtime. You can hardly blame her. Still . . . Dave was a pretty good guy. Is a pretty good guy, even if you won't get to see him much any more. Not perfect. You knew that all along, even if you aren't sure your daughter did. But pretty good. With the world the way it is, that's often more than enough.

Not this time. Too bad.

You raise your binoculars against these thoughts and this conversation. The Bushnells channel vision and attention away from dangerous places. Something—two somethings— swimming at the far end of the pool. Your right index finger slides to the center-focusing knob. "Ducks," you say, and then, nailing them, "Harlequin ducks."

"Where?" your daughter asks.

"Scan along the far bank till you see it poke out. They're just in front of that, a little to the left."

"I've got 'em," she says a moment later. "The male is nice."

"He is," you say. His head, blank and cinnamon with bold white spots, gives the ducks their name. "Everything's in breeding plumage up here."

"One more for the list," your daughter says. Harlequin ducks are life birds for both of you. Even in their duller winter feathers, they don't come down the Pacific coast as far as L.A. Your daughter's list is longer than yours. Not a lot, but it is. You've been birding since before she was born, but she goes at it with a passionate dedication you never found.

"Anything else?" you say. "Shall we go on?"

She's checking the south edge of the pool. When she spots something, she freezes. Then she laughs and lowers the binoculars. "Couple of white-crowns hopping around under the willows."

"Oh, boy." You've come 3,000 miles to see more of the cheeky little sparrows that mob your backyard feeders every winter.

Back into the car, then. You glance at the side-view mirror before pulling out. It's a big-city habit, more useful here than a third leg or a fifth wheel, but not much. Nothing coming either way as far as the eye can see. You're the only two people for miles.

"Pot—" your daughter starts. Too late. Thump. Your front teeth click together. "—hole."

Patches of snow—or is it ice?—lie on the hillsides. A little creek that runs down by the side of the road starts from one of them. Farther on, you come to a bridge over a real river. NO FISHING FROM BRIDGE, a sign in front of it says. You can barely make out the words. Plinkers have colandered the sign and chipped away a lot of enamel. What better place to plink than somewhere like this?

North and north again. You can't go faster than forty, not if you want to have any kidneys left at the end of the day. No hurry any which way. You stop every few miles to bird. Your daughter says she sees a hawk on some lichen-spattered rocks. You stop the car. You both get out.

"I think it's just another rock," you say. You raise the binoculars. It still looks like a rock. A dapper Lapland longspur hops near the bottom of the rockpile. He doesn't notice anything dangerous, either.

"It's a hawk," your daughter insists. The two of you walk towards it. It takes wing and flies off across the tundra. Your daughter grins. "Too small to be a peregrine or a gyrfalcon."

"Female merlin, I think," you say.

Her lips purse. She weighs size, color, shape. "Sounds right. That's another lifer for you, isn't it? I saw one up in Santa Barbara last year."

"One more checkmark in the Sibley," you say. A birder

without a guide is like a minister without a Bible. "You've got mosquitoes on your hat."

"Damn!" She taps the brim. Some of them fly off. Some stay put. She looks your way. "So do you, Dad."

You go through the same routine. Chances are it does the same amount of good—some, but not enough. You both try it again before you get back into the rental. You still have buzzing company after you close the doors. Your daughter squashes one mosquito after another against the inside of the windshield with a kleenex.

"There you go," you say.

She nails another one—maybe the last. Then she says, "Mom wouldn't have liked this part. She never could stand bugs."

"No." Your hands tighten on the wheel. Joints in palms and fingers twinge. Driving doesn't bother you most of the time, but you have to hold on tight here. You could let your daughter drive, but she makes a better spotter and navigator than you would. And you're used to driving when the two of you go somewhere together; you've been doing it since before she knew how.

Another river, wider than the last. You stop just beyond it. With running water, with trees and bushes on the banks, with mosquitoes and other insects buzzing above the stream and fish in it, rivers are great places for birds, and for birders. The scrubby willows here are trees, or almost; they're twelve, sometimes even fifteen, feet tall.

Something perches in the top of a distant one. Dark back, rusty belly . . . You swing your binoculars towards it as if they were a nineteenth-century naturalist's shotgun. "Varied thrush!"

"Where?" Your daughter's voice rises. This is another bird you both want.

You point it out to her. "You can see the black band across its breast."

She scans till she finds it. "I don't see that," she says slowly, and then, "Dad . . . it's got a yellow beak."

"No way!" But you look again. It does—and it doesn't have the black breastband you were sure it did. You saw what you wanted to see, not what was there. "Well, hell. I keep wanting varied thrushes, and I keep getting robins."

Till you got here, you hadn't thought they came to the tundra. They do, though. If anything, they're commoner here in the summertime than in Los Angeles. "Sorry, Dad," your daughter says.

"You were right. Don't be sorry for being right."

"Why not? Fat lot of good it's ever done me."

You can't find anything to say to that, so you look out over the river instead. An American golden plover in fancy black-and-white breeding plumage tiptoeing across a drift of pebbles makes a poor consolation prize. Your heart was set on a varied thrush, the way your stomach sometimes gets set on lamb chops. If the only thing in the freezer is ground round, you'll be disappointed no matter how good it turns out.

More mosquitoes get into the car with you. Your daughter commits insecticide as you drive north.

Off to the west rise the Kigluaik Mountains, purple streaked with white. More snow lingers on the northern slopes than the sunnier southern ones. The road winds by the north shore of Salmon Lake. You're forty miles out of Nome. There's a landing strip here, and a few cabins people use during the summer. You seem to have the place to yourselves now.

The rental car bumps across the dirt airstrip to the lakeshore. Two orange plastic cones mark the end of the strip. You stop just past them and get off. A breeze off the water keeps the mosquitoes down. Ducks swim in pairs: greater scaup, red-breasted mergansers.

Then something screeches furiously, about two feet above the crown of your hat. You can't help flinching. Graceful as a jet fighter, a black-capped bird with a red bill and feet rises and makes another pass at the two of you. *Screech!* You flinch again.

"Arctic tern." Your daughter does her best to sound matter-of-fact.

You manage a nod. "Sure is. We must be close to its nest."

Another furious dive-bomb, another skrawk from the tern. It doesn't hit either one of you, but it does its damnedest to drive you away. When you don't leave, it tries again and again. Other terns also screech, but only the one strafes you.

Your daughter is crying. You didn't see her start. "Hey," you say uselessly—tears always leave you helpless. "Hey. What is it?"

"Stupid bird." She tries to pretend this isn't happening, a losing proposition with wet streaks shining on her face. Almost too low for you to hear, she adds, "Families."

She and Dave had talked about starting one. They ended up talking to lawyers instead. It's a shame; you would have enjoyed grandchildren. But what can you do? Not much, not when she's so fragile that a bird defending its nest can set her off.

"Let's get out of here," she says roughly.

"Okay." You were married to her mother for almost forty years. Sometimes arguing only makes it worse.

The tern makes two more passes at the car as you drive away. You fear it will slam into the windshield, but it doesn't. You jounce across the airstrip to the road, which isn't much smoother. The Arctic tern has the lakeside to itself again.

"Sorry, Dad," your daughter says after a little while. "I didn't mean to drop that on you."

"Hey," you say one more time. Each of you should have had someone else. But there are no payoffs at the *should have had* window.

"I really thought—" Now your daughter breaks off. What did she think? That when she grew up she wouldn't need to go places with her father any more? Something like that, or she would have kept going. She could have; it wouldn't offend you. Of course people expect to do things on their own, or with a spouse, when they get into their thirties.

But life isn't what you expect. Life is what you get. And what your daughter's got is a birding trip to Nome with her old man.

Rattling up the Kougarok road would make anybody feel old. More scattered rocks off to the left give you another excuse to stop. "Let's see what we've got," you say. "Maybe we'll spot a wheatear."

Like the bluethroat, the northern wheatear is a Eurasian bird that visits western Alaska. It's supposed to display on rocks like those. With its dark mask, it looks a little like a shrike, but its black-and-white tail makes a terrific field mark. If you see one, you'll recognize it.

A cloud slides across the sun as soon as you get out of the car.

The breeze blows harder, down from the north. It may be summer, but you're only a hundred miles from the Arctic Circle. You zip up your anorak and tug on your hat to make sure it doesn't blow away. Through binoculars, the rocks scattered across the tundra seem close enough to touch. Motion on one makes you pause. But it's not a wheatear, only another American golden plover. You sweep some more.

Your daughter is looking toward the dwarf willows edging a puddle. Her scan suddenly stops, too. "What have you got?" you ask.

"Redpoll," she answers. "Just behind that little plant with the yellow flowers. See him? He's on one of the top branches."

"I've got him," you say. Redpolls are tiny birds, related to goldfinches. "Common or hoary, d'you think?"

"Common," she answers confidently. "Too dark to be a hoary." And when the bird flies off a few seconds later, it shows a striped rump. A hoary redpoll's rump would be white.

Along with the redpolls, white-crowns chirp in the willows and scratch under them. So do a couple of golden-crowned sparrows, white-crowns' less common cousins. You've seen them before, in the California hills. Your wife spotted one in the yard a few years ago, but you never have. She was so pleased. She was in remission then, too . . .

The sun comes out. The breeze fades. "That's more like it," you say, and unzip the coat again.

A moment later, you wonder how smart that is. As soon as the air grows still, the mosquitoes rise up around your daughter and you. Their hateful buzzing, like so many miniaturized dentist's drills, fills your ears. The repellent does its best. Not many land on your face or the back of your neck or your hands, the only flesh you're showing. But they perch in battalions on your hat and your clothes.

Your daughter, who is still scanning the rocks in hope of a wheatear, makes a disgusted noise. She turns the binoculars around and blows on one of the objective lenses. "Goddamn things are everywhere," she mutters.

"Want to go back to the car?"

"Yes." She slaps at her calf. Maybe one got in under the bottom of her jeans and went up above her sock. Or maybe it bit her through the sock. You wouldn't have thought a mosquito could, but you've never run into any like these before.

Your withdrawal across the tundra feels like Napoleon's after Moscow. "Good God!" you say when you reach the rental. You open the doors and close them again as fast as you can, but you still need some time to get rid of the mosquitoes you let in. Even then, a couple hover against the rear windows. If they stay back there, you'll let them live; going after them is more trouble than it's worth.

You pull onto the road again. "Man," your daughter says. You nod. One of the mosquitoes from the back comes forward. She squashes it. You smile at each other.

Mileposts on the Kougarok road are white numerals, written vertically, on a traffic-sign-green background. They're too small for plinkers to bother with. They're also too small to be easy to spot. When you see one, though, you can read it.

Your daughter calls them out. Sometimes she misses one, but she always gets the next if she does. She's reliable. If you say so, she'll tell you it's one more thing that doesn't do anybody any good. You keep quiet, hoping she'll know what you're thinking.

"Mile seventy," she says at last. "Getting close."

"Uh-huh." Your hands are twinging worse now. You take the right one off the wheel and open and close it a couple of times. Then you do the same with the left. Maybe it helps a little.

"Mile seventy-one," your daughter says. Half a minute later, she points. "There!"

"I see it." A pole, taller than one of the milepost supports, stabs into the tundra. Stuck to the top of it is what looks like the outer rim of a bicycle wheel. You wonder how it got there, and why. Did birders put it up? There's a marker like that at mile fifty-five on the Teller road, off to the west: a board in a roadside willow that points straight to the nest a pair of northern shrikes have built. This one is less precise, but it does the job.

You slow. A couple of hundred yards past the marker, a rutted track branches off the Kougarok road. It leads down into a little valley, with a creek chuckling over gravel at the bottom and with willow thickets all around.

"It's the right habitat for bluethroats," your daughter says. "They like running water, and they like willows."

Once upon a time, people lived down here, but not lately. The planking on the house and outbuildings to the right of the stream is weathered and pale. Glassless windows stare blackly, like the eye sockets of a skull. Willows grow right up to the doorways.

You drive as far as you can—half a mile or so—till the track turns to mud as it nears the stream. If you bog down in that, you may never get out, four-wheel drive or no. You stop. The map on the counter at the rental place says the bluethroats live farther down the valley, past the buildings and past an abandoned truck you haven't seen yet.

"Well." You open the door. "Let's see what we've got."

Your daughter slides out, too. "Oh, my God!" she says.

This may be the right habitat for bluethroats. It's the perfect habitat for mosquitoes. If a six-legged prophet preached of mosquito paradise, it would look like this. Plenty of little pools and puddles for eggs and larvae. All those willows to shelter the adults. No wind to speak of. And, now, sustenance.

The mosquitoes were bad on the open tundra. You don't want to believe how much worse they can be. "Oh, my *God*!" your daughter says again. She yanks the door open and snatches out the repellent. You spray each other once more.

It helps . . . some. But they're all over your clothes. And they buzz around the two of you in clouds as you walk down to the stream and then along it. You want to swat, but why bother? Would you swat a raindrop in a cloudburst?

You start to choke. Then you spit, and spit again. "Did you . . . inhale one?" your daughter asks.

"Not—quite." You spit one more time.

"Be careful here." She seems glad to change the subject. "Your shoes aren't waterproof." Hers are, bought from some fancy hikers' catalogue. You wear the old canvas-topped Adidases you always knock around in. They do let in water.

But you say, "My legs are longer than yours." The creek is only ten feet wide. Here and there, rocks and gravel stick up above the water. You cross behind her without getting wet.

The ground is a little better over there. But the willows—hardly any taller than you are—press close to the bank. The air around you is curtained with mosquitoes.

You walk on. A mosquito lands on your ear. You brush it away. A bird darts across the stream and into the willows. It's here and gone before you can ID it. "Was it—?" you ask at the same time as your daughter says, "It could have been—"

It starts to sing. That lets you get a fix on it. Two pairs of binoculars swing its way.

"Redpoll," you say together, and lower the binoculars with identical sighs.

"Map said they were farther down." Is your daughter boosting her spirits or yours?

"We'll see." You have to cross the stream again; the willows press right down to the waterline. You manage to stay dry once more. Here in this sheltered place, it's almost warm. Your daughter takes off her outer sweater and ties it around her waist. You unzip your jacket again.

You go up to the abandoned house to see if a hawk or, more likely, an owl is nesting inside. You give your eyes a chance to get used to the darkness inside, but you don't see anything. Reluctantly, you decide there's nothing to see.

Your daughter points. "There's the truck, Dad!"

"Where?" you say, not spotting it. Then you do. "Boy, that's about as abandoned as it gets."

How many years has it squatted there? Long enough for rain and snow and ice to have had their way with its paint. Rust covers every inch of the chassis. The dark red-brown blends perfectly with the dirt and with the green and brown of the willows growing alongside. You and your daughter fight through the shrubby willows for a closer look. The side windows are either rolled down all the way or long gone. Cracks craze the windshield and smaller rear window.

Mosquitoes hum all around. You breathe in another one. By now, you have practice at this—you spit it out without your daughter's even noticing.

"Past the dead truck. That's what's on the map." Excitement brightens her voice. The map might point toward buried treasure on the Spanish Main, not bluethroat nests in the middle of the Seward Peninsula.

A lot of maps that said they pointed toward treasure on the Spanish Main really pointed toward nothing. You have to hope this one won't be like that. People have more incentive to lie about doubloons and pieces of eight than about little thrushes from Asia . . . don't they?

You'll find out. You follow the creek another couple of hundred yards. You stop in a small clearing. "If they're anywhere, they're here," you say.

"Sure." Your daughter still sounds more confident than you feel. If she can still believe things will work out for the best in this best of all possible worlds, more power to her.

She raises her binoculars and slowly scans the closer willows, then the more distant ones. You do the same. You've come all this way. Long odds you'll ever get here again. You'd be an idiot not to give it your best shot.

Which doesn't mean you'll get what you're after. Your wife gave it her best shot, God knows. So did your daughter. So did her ex, even if she so doesn't want to hear that.

You lower the binoculars and look around. Something's perched in a willow up near the edge of the valley. Your daughter's already spotted it. You raise the field glasses again and aim them that way. "What do you think?" you ask her.

She sighs. "It's an American tree sparrow. Right size, wrong bird."

You take a longer look. You sigh, too, because she's right. She usually is. The cinnamon crown, the dark spot on the breast, the bill that's dark above and yellowish below . . . American tree sparrow, all right. The first time you saw one here, it was a life bird for both of you, because it's rare along the West Coast. But it's common here in the summertime, and in the upper Midwest and East during the winter. Not a bluethroat. Not even close.

You scan some more. You spot a Wilson's warbler: a little yellow bird with a black cap. The last one you saw was hopping around the magnolia in your own back yard.

After a while, you say, "We ought to head back to the car."

"I know." Your daughter doesn't budge. "I hate to give up, though."

"So do I. Still, if we were going to find anything . . . "

"Pish! Pish! Pish!" Your daughter doesn't say that to you. It's a noise birders make to lure shy birds out of cover. Sometimes—not very often, in your experience—it works. Birders who do it too much are called pishers. For anyone with even a little Yiddish, that's funny. "Pish! Pish! Pish!" Your daughter isn't a pisher, but she'll try whatever she can.

Nothing comes out of the willows. Only mosquitoes fly around you. You take a couple of steps in the direction of the car. Your daughter's stiff back says she doesn't want to see you.

"Come on," you say. "We'll bird all the way there. Maybe we'll find one."

"Maybe." She closes up with you. Then she leans toward the willows again. "Pish! Pish! Pish!"

"Pish! Pish! Pish!" You even try it yourself. Why not? What have you got to lose? "Pish! Pish! Pish!" A fighting retreat.

Stop and pish. Stop and scan. Back past the truck carcass. Past the buildings. Through the mosquitoes. Despite the repellent, they do land. How many bites will you end up with? You won't feel them till later.

You see another redpoll, or maybe the same one again. A golden-crowned sparrow is bathing in the creek, fluttering its wings to flip water onto its back.

"Stupid thing." Your daughter is mad at it for not being a bluethroat.

"We tried our best," you say. You remember your wife. Sometimes it just isn't good enough.

There's the rental car. You look around one more time. The bluethroats aren't supposed to be here, so close to the main road. But they aren't where they're supposed to be, so what the hell? A bird in the willows . . . is another American tree sparrow. You don't need your daughter to identify this one for you.

She sees it, too, and what it is. She shakes her head and lowers her binoculars.

You open the door and quickly slide in. Your daughter does the same thing on the passenger side. You both kill some of the mosquitoes that got in with you. Then you start the car. You turn around carefully on the narrow track. Back toward the road. Back toward Nome.

Maybe, behind you now, the bluethroats flit through the willow branches. Maybe they snatch mosquitoes out of the air and carry them back to hungry hatchlings in their nests. Maybe they were never there at all.

WORLDS ENOUGH, AND TIME

I've been interested in ecological invasions and in what people call the Cambrian explosion for a long time. This little piece originally appeared as a "Probability Zero" in *Analog*. Zero? I don't know. Have you got a better explanation?

*S*O MANY WORLDS, SO LITTLE TIME, SAID THE SLIGHTLY scorched sticker on the side of the starship.

This one had an oxygen atmosphere, but not much else going for it. The oxygen meant there were plants in the seas. The ship's database said those seas held animals, too: wormy things crawling on the mud, maybe digging into it; blobby things floating in the water. That was about it.

On land? Nothing. Zero. Zip. Zilch. Bare rock. The chewed-up bare rock that's called dirt. No trees. No flowers. No grass. No ferny things. No mossy things, even. No nothing. Certainly nothing scurrying over the ground or buzzing through the air.

Sometimes planets like this had a stark beauty. The father liked such worlds, which was why they'd stopped at this one. But he'd flitted here, and he'd flitted there, and he had to say he was disappointed.

The mother wasn't. She hadn't much wanted to come here in the first place. But they'd been married a long time. If you expected him to give a little, you had to do the same.

They stood side by side, watching the ocean lap against a tropical—but bare, utterly bare—beach. He sighed. "I've seen about enough," he said. "It . . . just isn't quite what I hoped for."

Told you so. But she didn't say it. They *had* been married a long time. All she said was, "I wouldn't mind seeing something different."

"We'll do that, then," he said.

He was just turning back toward the ship when the kids swarmed down the ladder and ran toward him. That was a prodigy of sorts. The kids cared more about their games and the aquarium than about seeing what they thought of as a dull old planet. Well, by now he thought of it the same way, which was the problem.

"What's up?" he asked.

"Aquarium's in trouble," the girl said.

"Environmental unit crapped out," the boy agreed. He'd head off to the university after they got home. Where did time go?

"Well, plug in the replacement," the father said.

They both looked shamefaced. "We forgot to pack one," the girl said.

"Oh, dear," the mother said.

"Without an environmental unit, everything'll die." By the way the boy looked at the father, it was somehow *his* fault.

"I like the critters in there. I really like them." The girl sounded heartbroken.

"I don't know what to tell you." The father knew damn well it *wasn't* his fault.

The girl pointed toward the sea that seemed to stretch forever. "Could we . . . give them a chance, anyway? Not just watch them die?"

"It's against the rules," the father said doubtfully.

"*Please!*" the kids chorused.

"I'll never tell," the mother added. "Who's to know?"

"Well . . . " He thought a minute, then shrugged. "Okay—

go ahead. But keep your mouths shut after we get home, you hear?"

"You're the greatest, Dad!" the boy said. He and the girl ran back toward the ship.

JACK CONWAY FIRED UP HIS MAC AND STARTED THE POWER-Point presentation. A projector put one weird creature after another up on the big screen. "This is a trilobite—an early arthropod. Some of you probably recognize it," Jack told his class. "This is *Selkirkia*, a priapulid worm. It lived in the mud, as they still do.... This is *Aysheia*, a lobopod. Looks something like a worm and something like a bug, doesn't it? . . . *Hallucigenia*—great name—is probably another lobopod, with protective spines . . . *Canadia* is an annelid, related to earthworms . . . And this little fishy thing with eyestalks or antennae or whatever they are is *Pikaia*, an early chordate—somebody from our own phylum."

He paused. "Nobody quite knows why there was such an explosion of metazoan body plans at the beginning of the Cambrian, 543 million years ago. Some of the more interesting theories include . . . "

HE WOKE IN DARKNESS

I don't quite know what you'd call this story. Dark fantasy? Horror? Something in there. Not a place I seem to go very often, but I did this time. The other line that occurs to me is from Marlow: *Why this is hell, nor am I out of it.*

H E WOKE IN DARKNESS, NOT KNOWING WHO HE WAS. THE taste of earth filled his mouth.

It shouldn't have ended this way. He knew that, though he couldn't say how or why. He couldn't even say what *this way* was, not for sure. He just knew it was wrong. He'd always understood about right and wrong, as far back as he could remember.

How far back was that? Why, it was . . . as far as it was. He didn't know exactly how far. That seemed wrong, too, but he couldn't say why.

Darkness lay heavily on him, unpierced, unpierceable. It wasn't the dark of night, nor even the dark of a closed and shuttered room at midnight. No light had ever come here. No light ever would, or could. Not the darkness of a mineshaft. The darkness of . . . the tomb?

Realizing he must be dead made a lot of things fall together. A lot, but not enough. As far back as he could remember . . . He couldn't remember *dying*, dammit. Absurdly, that made him angry. Something so important in a man's life, you'd think he would remember it. But he didn't, and he didn't know what he could do about it.

He would have laughed, there in the darkness, if only he could. He hadn't expected Afterwards to be like this. He didn't know how he'd expected it to be, but not like this. Again, though, what could he do about it?

I can remember. I can try to remember, anyways. Again, he would have laughed if he could. *Why the hell not? I've got all the time in the world.*

LIGHT. AN EXPLOSION OF LIGHT. AFTERNOON SUNSHINE BLASTing through the dirty, streaky windshield of the beat-up old Ford station wagon bouncing west down Highway 16 toward Philadelphia.

A bigger explosion of light inside his mind. A name! He had a name! He was Cecil, Cecil Price, Cecil Ray Price. He knew it like . . . like a man knows his name, that's how. That time without light, without self? *A dream*, he told himself. *Must have been a dream.*

Those were his hands on the wheel, pink and square and hard from years of labor in the fields. He was only twenty-seven, but he'd already done a lifetime's worth of hard work. It felt like a long lifetime's worth, too.

He took one hand off the wheel for a second to run it through his brown hair, already falling back at the temples. Had he dozed for a second while he was driving? He didn't think so, but what else could it have been? Lucky he didn't drive the wagon off the road into the cotton fields, into the red dirt.

They would love that. They would laugh their asses off. Well, they weren't going to get the chance.

Sweat ran down his face. His clothes felt welded to him. The air was thick with water, damn near thick enough to slice. The start of summer in Mississippi. It would stay like this for months.

He had the window open to give himself a breeze. It didn't help much. When it got this hot and sticky, nothing helped much. He ran his hand through his hair again, to try to keep it out of his eyes.

"You all right, Cecil?" That was Muhammad Shabazz. Along with Tariq Abdul-Rashid, he crouched down in the back seat. The two young Black Muslims didn't want the law, or what passed for the law in Mississippi in 1964, spotting them. They'd come down from the North to give the oppressed and disenfranchised whites in the state a helping hand, and the powers that be hated them worse than anybody.

"I'm okay," Cecil Price answered. *I'm okay now*, he thought. *I know who I am. Hell, I know that I am.* He shook his head. That moment of lightless namelessness was fading, and a good thing, too.

"We get to Meridian, everything'll be fine," Muhammad Shabazz said.

"Sure," Cecil said. "Sure." The night before, the locals had torched a white church over by Longdale. He'd taken the Northern blacks over there to do what they could for the congregation. Now . . .

Now they had to get through Neshoba County. They had to get past Philadelphia. They had to run the gauntlet of lawmen who hated white people and Black Knights of Voodoo who hated whites even more—and of lawmen who *were* Black Knights of Voodoo and hated whites most of all. And they had to do it in the Racial Alliance for Complete Equality's beat-up station wagon. If RACE's old blue Ford wasn't the best-known car in eastern Mississippi, Price was damned if he knew another one that would be.

Of course, he might be damned any which way. So might the two idealistic young Negroes who'd come down from New York and Ohio to give his downtrodden race a hand. If the law spotted this much too spottable car . . .

Cecil Price wished he hadn't had that thought right then, in the instant before he saw the flashing red light in his rear-view mirror, in the instant before he heard the siren's scream. Panic stabbed at him. "What do I do?" he said hoarsely. He wanted to floor the gas pedal. He wanted to, but he didn't. The main thing that held him back was the certain knowledge that the old wagon couldn't break sixty unless you flung it off a cliff.

"Pull over." Muhammad Shabazz's voice was calm. "Don't let 'em get us for evading arrest or any real charge. We haven't done anything wrong, so they can't do anything to us."

"You sure of that, man?" Tariq Abdul-Rashid sounded nervous.

"This is all about the rule of law," Muhammad Shabazz said patiently. "For us, for them, for everybody."

He respected the rule of law. It meant more to him than anything else. Cecil Price could only hope it meant something to the man in the car with the light and the siren. He could hope so, yeah. Could he believe it? That was a different story.

But Price didn't see that he had any choice here. He pulled off onto the shoulder. The brakes squeaked as he brought the blue Ford to a stop. Pebbles rattled against the car's underpanels. Red dust swirled up around it.

The black-and-white pulled up behind the Ford. A great big Negro in a deputy sheriff's uniform got out and swaggered up toward the station wagon. Cecil Price watched him in the mirror, not wanting to turn around. That arrogant strut—and the pistol in the lawman's hand—spoke volumes about the way things in Mississippi had been since time out of mind.

Coming up to the driver's-side door, the sheriff peered in through sunglasses that made him look more like a machine, a hate-driven machine, than a man. "Son of a bitch!" he exploded. "*You* ain't Larry Rainey!"

"No, sir," Price said. Part of that deference was RACE training—don't give the authorities an excuse to beat on you. And part of it was drilled into whites in the South from the time they could toddle and lisp. If they *didn't* show respect, they often didn't live to get a whole lot older than that.

Larry Rainey was older than Cecil Price and smarter than Cecil and tougher than Cecil, too. He'd been in RACE a lot longer than Cecil had. The Black Knights of Voodoo probably hated him more than any other white man from this part of the state.

But the way they hated Larry Rainey was like nothing next to the way they hated what they called the black agitators from the North. Even behind the deputy sheriff's shades, Cecil could see his eyes widen when he got a look at Muhammad Shabazz and Tariq Abdul-Rashid. "Well, well!" he boomed, the way a man with a shotgun will when a couple of big, fat ducks fly right over his blind. "Looky what we got here! We got us a couple of buckra-lovin' ragheads!"

"Sheriff," Muhammad Shabazz said tightly. He didn't wear a turban, and never had. Neither did Tariq Abdul-Rashid, who nodded like somebody trying hard not to show how scared he was. Cecil Price was scared, too, damn near scared shitless, and hoped the black man with the gun and the Smokey-the-Bear hat couldn't tell.

The deputy went on as if the Black Muslim hadn't spoken: "We got us a couple of Northern radicals who reckon they're better'n other folks their color, so they can hop on a bus and come down here and tell us how to live. And we got us one uppity buckra, too, sneakin' around and stirrin' up what oughta be damn well left alone. Well, I got news for y'all. That don't fly, not in Neshoba County it don't. What the hell you doin' here, anyway?"

"We were looking at what's left of Mount Zion Church in Longdale," Muhammad Shabazz answered.

"Yeah, I just bet you were. Fat lot your kind cares about churches," the big black deputy jeered.

"We care about justice, sir." Muhammad Shabazz spoke with respect that didn't come close to hiding the anger underneath. "I do, and Mr. Abdul-Rashid does, and Mr. Price does, too. Do you, sir? Does justice mean anything to you at all?"

"It means I know better'n to call a lousy, lazy, no-account buckra *Mister*. Ain't that right, Cecil?" When Price didn't answer fast enough to suit the deputy sheriff, the man stuck the pistol in his face and roared, *"Ain't that right, boy?"*

Muhammad Shabazz had nerve. If he didn't have nerve, he never would have ridden down to Mississippi from Cleveland in the first place. "We didn't do anything wrong, sir," he told the deputy. "We didn't even break any traffic laws. You have no good reason to pull us over. Why aren't you investigating real crimes, like a firebombed church?"

To Cecil Price's amazement, the deputy smiled the broadest,

nastiest, wickedest smile he'd ever seen, and he'd seen some lulus. "What do you reckon I'm doin'?" he said. "What the hell do you reckon I'm doin'? All three of you sons of bitches are under arrest for suspicion of arson. A charge like that, you can rot in jail the rest of your worthless lives. Serve y'all right, too, you want to know what I think."

"You're out of your mind," Muhammad Shabazz exclaimed.

"We wouldn't burn a church," Tariq Abdul-Rashid agreed, startled out of his frightened silence. "That *is* crazy."

"We've got no reason to do anything like that. Why would we, sir?" Cecil Price tried to make the deputy forget his comrades didn't stay polite.

It didn't work. He might have known it wouldn't. Hell, he had known it wouldn't. "Why? I'll tell you why," the Negro in the lawman's uniform said. "So decent, God-fearing folks get blamed for it, that's why. You agitators'll try and pin it all on us, make us look bad on the TV, give the federal government an excuse to stick its nose in affairs that ain't none of its business and never will be. So hell, yes, you're under arrest. Suspicion of arson, like I said. I'll throw your sorry asses in jail right now. You drive on into Philadelphia quiet-like, or you gonna do something stupid like try and escape?"

Cecil Price didn't need to be a college-educated fellow like the two blacks in the car with him to know what that meant. *You do anything but drive straight to jail and I'll kill all of you.* "I won't do anything dumb," he told the deputy.

"Better not, boy, or it's the last fuckup you ever pull." The big black man threw back his head and laughed. "Unless you already pulled your last one, that is." Laughing still, he walked back to the black-and-white. He opened the door, got in—the shocks sagged under his bulk—and slammed it shut.

"Let him jail us on that stupid trumped-up charge," Muhammad Shabazz said as Price started the Ford's engine. "It'll do just as much to help the cause as the church bombing."

"I hope you're right," Price said, pulling back onto the highway, "but he's a mean one. The Neshoba County Sheriff's meaner, but the deputy's bad enough and then some."

"You think he's BKV?" Tariq Abdul-Rashid asked.

"Black Knights of Voodoo?" Price shrugged. "I don't know for sure, but I wouldn't be surprised if he goes night-riding with a mask and a shield and a spear."

In Philadelphia, a few people stared at the car with the white and the two blacks in it. Cecil Price didn't care for those stares, not even a little bit. He didn't care for any part of what was going on, but he couldn't do thing one about it. He parked in front of the jail. The deputy's car pulled up right behind the RACE wagon.

Another black deputy sat behind the front desk when Price and Muhammad Shabazz and Tariq Abdul-Rashid walked into the jail. "What the hell's goin' on here?" he asked the man who'd arrested the civil-rights workers.

"Suspicion of arson," the first deputy answered. "I reckon they must've had somethin' to do with torchin' the white folks' church over by Longdale."

"That's the—" What was the man behind the desk about to say? *That's the silliest goddamn thing I ever heard*? Something like that—Cecil Price was sure of it. But then the other Negro's eyes narrowed. "Fuck me," he said, and pointed first to

Muhammad Shabazz and then to Tariq Abdul-Rashid. "Ain't these the raghead bastards who came down from the North to raise trouble?"

"That's them, all right," said the deputy who'd arrested them. "And this here buckra's Cecil Price. I thought at first I got me Larry Rainey—you know how all these white folks look alike. But what the hell? If you can't grab a big fish, a little fish'll do."

"That's a fact," said the deputy behind the desk. "That sure as hell is a fact, all right. Yeah, lock 'em up. We can figure out what to do with 'em later."

"You betcha." The first deputy marched his prisoners to the cells farther back in the jail. "In here, you two," he told Muhammad Shabazz and Tariq Abdul-Rashid, and herded them into the first cell on the right. He stuck Cecil Price in the second cell on the right. Even at a time like this, even in a situation like this, he never thought to put a white man in with Negroes. That was part of what was wrong in Philadelphia, right there.

After Price and Muhammad Shabazz and Tariq Abdul-Rashid were safely locked away, the man who'd arrested them clumped up the corridor and then out the front door. "Where you goin'?" called the man behind the desk.

"Got to see the Priest," the first deputy answered. "Anybody asks after those assholes, you never seen 'em, you never heard nothin' about 'em. You got that?"

"All right by me," the other deputy said. The first one slammed the door after him as he went out. He seemed to have to slam any door he came to.

Cecil Price had only thought he was scared shitless before. Not letting anybody know he and his friends were in jail was bad. Going to see the Priest was a hell of a lot worse. The Priest was a tall, scrawny, bald black man who hated whites with a fierce and simple passion. He was also the chief Neshoba County recruiting officer for the Black Knights of Voodoo. Trouble followed him the way thunder followed lightning.

Price wondered whether Muhammad Shabazz and Tariq Abdul-Rashid knew enough to be as frightened as he was. The Priest had been trouble for years, while they'd been down here only a couple of months. The Priest would still be trouble long after they went back to the North . . . if they ever got the chance to go North again.

It must have been about half past five when the phone at the front desk jangled loudly. "Neshoba County Jail," the deputy there said. He paused to listen, then went on, "No, I ain't seen 'em. Jesus Christ! You lose your garbage, you expect me to go pickin' it up for you?" He slammed the phone down again.

"Deputy!" Muhammad Shabazz called through the bars of his cell. "Deputy, can I speak to you for a minute?"

A scrape of chair legs against cheap linoleum. Slow, heavy, arrogant footsteps. A deep, angry voice: "What the hell you want?"

"I'd like to make a telephone call, please."

A pause. Cecil Price looked out of his cell just in time to see the deputy sheriff shake his head. His big, round belly shook, too, but it didn't remind Price of a bowlful of jelly—more of a wrecking ball that would smash anything in its way. "No, I don't reckon so," he said. "You ain't callin' nobody."

"I have a constitutional right to make a telephone call," Muhammad Shabazz insisted, politely but firmly.

"Don't you give me none of your Northern bullshit," the Negro deputy said. "Constitution doesn't say jack shit about telephone calls. How could it? No telephones when they wrote the damn thing, were there? *Were* there, you smartass cocksucker?"

"No, but—" Muhammad Shabazz broke off.

"Constitutional right, my ass," the deputy sheriff said. "You got a constitutional right to get what's comin' to you, and you will. You just bet you will." He lumbered back to the desk.

In a low voice, Cecil Price said, "We're in deep now."

"No kidding." Muhammad Shabazz sounded like a man who wanted to make a joke but was too worried to bring it off.

"They aren't gonna let us out of here," Tariq Abdul-Rashid said. "Not in one piece, they aren't."

"We'll see what happens, that's all," Muhammad Shabazz said. "They can't think they'll get away with it." To Cecil Price, that only proved the man who'd come down from the North didn't understand how things really worked in Mississippi. Of course the deputy sheriffs thought they'd get away with it. Why wouldn't they? Blacks had been getting away with things against whites who stepped out of line ever since slavery days. Times were starting to change; Negroes of goodwill like Muhammad Shabazz and Tariq Abdul-Rashid were helping to make them change. But they hadn't changed yet—and the deputies and their pals were determined they wouldn't change no matter what. And so . . .

And so we're in deep for sure, Cecil Price thought, fighting despair.

＝◆＝

THE FIRST DEPUTY SHERIFF, THE ONE WHO'D ARRESTED THEM, returned to the jail not long after the sun went down. He walked back to the cells to look at the prisoners, laughed a gloating laugh, and then went up front again.

"What's the Priest got to say?" asked the man at the front desk.

"It's all taken care of," the first deputy answered.

"They comin' here?"

"Nah." The first deputy sounded faintly disappointed. "It'd be too damn raw. We'd end up with the fuckin' feds on our case for sure."

"What's going on, then?"

The first deputy told him. He pitched his voice too low to let Cecil Price make it out. By the way the desk man laughed, he thought it was pretty good. Price was sure *he* wouldn't.

Time crawled by on hands and knees. The phone rang once, but it had nothing to do with Price and Muhammad Shabazz and Tariq Abdul-Rashid. It was a woman calling to find out if her no-account husband was sleeping off another binge in the drunk tank. He wasn't. But it only went to show that, despite the struggle for whites' civil rights, ordinary life in Philadelphia went on.

Around half past ten, the first deputy came tramping back to the cells again. To Cecil Price's amazement, he had a jingling bunch of keys on a big brass key ring with him. He opened the door to Price's cell. "Come on out, boy," he said. "Reckon I've got to turn you loose."

Price wanted to stick a finger in his ear to make sure he'd heard right. "You sure?" he blurted.

"Yeah, I'm sure," the deputy said. "I been askin' around. You weren't at the church when it went up. Neither were these assholes." He pointed into the cell that held Muhammad Shabazz and Tariq Abdul-Rashid. "Gotta let them go, too, dammit."

"You'll hear from our lawyers," Muhammad Shabazz promised. "False arrest is false arrest, even if you think twice about it later. This is still a free country, whether you know it or not."

Although Cecil Price agreed with every word he said, he wished the Black Muslim would shut the hell up. Pissing off the deputy right when he was letting them out of jail wasn't the smartest move in the world, not even close. But Price walked out of his cell. A moment later, Muhammad Shabazz and Tariq Abdul-Rashid walked out of theirs, too.

The deputy with the wrecking-ball belly at the front desk gave them back their wallets and keys and pocket change. "If you're smart, you'll get your white ass outa Philadelphia. Go on down to Meridian and never come back," he told Cecil Price. "You cause trouble around here again, you look at a black woman walkin' down the street around here again, you show your ugly buckra face around here again, you are fuckin' dead meat. You hear me?"

"Oh, yes, sir. I sure do hear you," Cecil Price said. That was how you played the game in Mississippi. Price hadn't promised to do one thing the deputy said. But he'd heard him, all right. He couldn't very well not have heard him.

"Go on, then. Get lost."

The first deputy walked out into the muggy night with the white man and the two Northern blacks. A mosquito buzzed around Price's ear. Price slapped at it. The deputy laughed. He watched while Price and the Black Muslims got into RACE's blue Ford wagon. Price started up the car. The deputy went on watching as he put it in gear and drove away. In the rear-view mirror, Price watched him walk back into the Neshoba County Jail.

"Maybe they really are learning they can't pull crap like that on us," Tariq Abdul-Rashid said.

"Don't bet on it," was Muhammad Shabazz's laconic response. "They don't back up unless they've got a reason to back up. Isn't that right, Cecil? . . . Cecil?"

Cecil Price didn't answer, not right away. His eyes were on the rear-view mirror again. He didn't like what he saw. This time of night, driving out of a little town like Philadelphia, they should have had the road to themselves. They should have, but they didn't. One, then two, sets of headlights followed them out of town. Price stepped on the gas. If those cars back there weren't interested in him and his black friends, he'd lose them.

"Hey, man, take it easy," Tariq Abdul-Rashid said. "You don't want to give the law a chance to run us in for speeding."

"We've got company back there," Price said. Speeding up hadn't shaken those two cars. If anything, they were closer. And a third set of headlights was coming out of Philadelphia, zooming down Highway 19 like a bat out of hell.

Tariq Abdul-Rashid and Muhammad Shabazz looked back over their shoulder. "You think they're on our tail, Cecil?" Tariq Abdul-Rashid asked.

Before Price could say anything, Muhammad Shabazz said everything that needed saying: "Gun it! Gun it like a son of a bitch!"

The old Ford's motor should have roared when Cecil Price jammed the pedal to the metal. Instead, it groaned and grunted. Yeah, the wagon went faster, but it didn't go faster fast enough. The two pairs of headlights behind the Ford got bigger and bigger, brighter and brighter, closer and closer. And the third pair, the set that got the late start, might almost have been flying along Highway 19. That was one souped-up set of wheels, and the rustbucket Price was driving didn't have a prayer of staying ahead. Before long, whoever was driving that hot machine got right on the wagon's tail.

Desperate now, Price killed his lights and made a screeching, sliding right onto Highway 492. Only in Mississippi, he thought, would such a miserable chunk of asphalt merit the name of highway. But if it let him shake his pursuers, he would bless its undeserved name forevermore.

Only it didn't. The lead pursuer, the hopped-up car that had come zooming out of Philadelphia, also made the turn. Even over the growl of his own car's engine, Cecil Price could hear its brakes screech as it clawed around the corner. Then the pursuer's siren came on and the red light on top of the roof began to flash.

"Jesus! It's that damn deputy again!" Price said. "What am I gonna do?"

"Can we outrun him?" Muhammad Shabazz asked as the beat-up Ford bucketed down the road.

"Not a chance in hell," Price answered. "He's liable to start shooting at us if I don't stop." If he got hit, or if a tire got hit, the car would fly off the road and burst into flames. That was a bad way to go.

"Maybe you better stop," Tariq Abdul-Rashid said.

"Damned if I do and damned if I don't," Cecil Price said bitterly, but his foot had already found the brake pedal. The old blue station wagon slowed, stopped.

The deputy sheriff's car stopped behind it, the same way it had earlier that day. This time, though, the other two cars also stopped. The big black buck of a deputy sheriff got out of his car and strode up to the Ford wagon. "I thought you were going back to Meridian if we let you out of jail."

"We were," Price answered.

"Well, you sure were taking the long way around. Get out of that car," the deputy said. That was the last thing Cecil Price wanted to do. But he thought the deputy would shoot him and the two Black Muslims right there if they refused. Reluctantly, he obeyed. Perhaps even more reluctantly, Muhammad Shabazz and Tariq Abdul-Rashid followed him.

Men were also getting out of the two cars stopped behind the deputy's. Price's heart sank when he saw them. There was the Priest, all right, black as the ace of spades. And there were ten or twelve other Negroes with him. Price recognized some of them as BKV men. He didn't know for sure that the others were, but what else would they be? Some had guns. Others carried crowbars or tire irons or Louisville Sluggers. They all wore rubber gloves so they wouldn't leave fingerprints.

"You don't want to do this," Muhammad Shabazz said earnestly. "I'm telling you the truth—you don't. It won't get you what you think it will."

"Shut the fuck up, you goddamn raghead race traitor." The deputy sheriff's voice was hard and cold as iron. "You get in the back of my car now, you hear?"

"What will you do to us?" Tariq Abdul-Rashid asked.

"Whatever it is, we'll do it right here and right now if you don't shut the fuck up and do like you're told," the deputy answered. "Now stop mouthing off and move, damn you."

Numbly, as if caught in a bad dream, Cecil Price and his companions got into the back of the deputy sheriff's car. A steel grating walled them off from the front seat. Neither back door had a lock or a door handle on the inside. Once you went in there, you stayed in there till somebody decided to let you out.

The deputy slid behind the wheel again. The men from the Black Knights of Voodoo got back into their cars, too. A couple of them aimed weapons at Cecil Price and the Black Muslims before they did. The deputy sheriff waved the BKV men away. "Not quite time yet," he told them.

"This won't help you. The country won't be proud of you. They'll go after you like you wouldn't believe," Muhammad Shabazz said. "If you hurt us, you help our side, and that's nothing but the truth."

"I don't want to listen to your bullshit, you buckra-lovin' raghead, and *that's* nothin' but the truth," the deputy said. "So maybe you just better shut the fuck up."

"Why? What difference does it make now?" the Black Muslim asked.

Instead of answering, the deputy sheriff put the car in gear. He made a Y-turn—the road was too narrow for a U—and swung back around the cars full of BKV men. Then he hit the brakes to wait while they turned around, too. *Good cooperation in a bad cause*, Cecil Price thought. If RACE members worked together as smoothly as these BKV bastards . . .

"All right," the deputy muttered, and the black-and-white moved forward again. Now that he wasn't chasing people at top speed, the deputy sheriff acted like a careful driver. He flicked the turn signal before making a left back onto Highway 19. *Click! Click! Click!* The sound seemed very loud inside the passenger compartment. What went through Price's mind was, *Measuring off the seconds left in my life.*

As soon as the deputy finished the turn, of course, the clicking stopped. Price wished his mind had been going in some other direction a moment before. The deputy drove toward Philadelphia for a minute or two, then used the turn signal again. *Click! Click! Click!* Cecil Price cherished and dreaded the sound of those passing seconds, both at the same time. He grimaced when the deputy finished the new left turn and the indicator fell silent again.

"Where the hell are we?" Muhammad Shabazz muttered.

Before Price could answer him, the deputy did: "This here is Rock Cut Road. Ain't hardly anything around these parts. That's how come we're here."

"Oh, shit," Tariq Abdul-Rashid said. Price couldn't have put it better himself.

The deputy wasn't kidding. Looking out the car's dirty windows, Price saw nothing but a narrow red dirt road and weed-filled fields to either side. Behind the black-and-white, car doors slammed as the Black Knights of Voodoo got out and advanced.

"I'm gonna open the door and let y'all out now," the deputy said. "You don't want to do anything stupid, you hear?"

"What the hell difference does it make at this stage of things?" Tariq Abdul-Rashid asked.

"Well, some things are gonna happen. They're gonna, and I don't reckon anything'll change that," the deputy sheriff said seriously. "But they can happen easy, you might say, or they can happen not so easy. You won't like it if they happen not so easy. Believe you me, you won't, not even a little bit."

He got out of the car. *Can we jump him when he opens the door?* Price wondered. He shook his head. Not a chance in church. Not a chance in hell.

One more *click!*: the door opening. Heart racing a mile a minute, legs feather-light with fear, Cecil Price got out of the Neshoba County Sheriff's Department car. The dirt scraped and crunched under the soles of his shoes. *Is that the last thing I'll ever feel?* It didn't seem like enough.

Two Black Knights of Voodoo grabbed Tariq Abdul-Rashid. Two others seized Muhammad Shabazz, and two more laid hold of Cecil Price. Another BKV man walked up to Tariq Abdul-Rashid, pistol in hand. The headlights of the cars behind the black-and-white picked out the globe and anchor tattooed on his right biceps.

"Go get 'em, Wayne," somebody said in a low, hoarse voice— the Priest, Cecil Price saw.

"I will, goddammit. I will," answered the BKV man with the pistol. Price happened to know that Wayne Roberts, in spite of the tattoo, had been dishonorably discharged from the Marine Corps. In the Black Knights of Voodoo, though, he could be a big man.

He scowled at Tariq Abdul-Rashid. "No," the Black Muslim whispered. "Please, no."

"Fuck you, man," Roberts said. "You ain't nothin' but a stinkin' buckra in a black skin." He thumbed back the revolver's hammer and pulled the trigger.

The roar was amazingly loud. The bullet, from point-blank range, caught Tariq Abdul-Rashid in the middle of the forehead. He went limp all at once, as if his bones had turned to water. "Way to go, Wayne!" said one of the men who held him. When his captors let go, he flopped down like a sack of beans, dead before he hit the ground.

"You see?" the black deputy said. "Hard or easy. That there was pretty goddamn easy, wasn't it?"

The BKV men who had hold of Muhammad Shabazz dragged him forward. Even as they did, he was trying to talk sense to them. "I understand how you feel, but this won't help you," he said in a calm, reasonable voice. "Killing us won't do anything for your cause. You—"

"Shut up, asshole." Wayne Roberts cuffed him across the face. "You bet this'll do us some good. We'll be rid of *you*, won't we? Good riddance to bad rubbish." He shot Muhammad Shabazz the same way he'd killed the other Black Muslim.

"Easy as can be," the deputy sheriff said. "Easier'n he deserved, I reckon. Motherfucker never knew what hit him." The hot, wet air was thick with the stinks of smokeless powder, of blood, of shit, of fear, of rage.

Easy or not, Cecil Price didn't want to die. With a sudden shout that even startled him, he broke loose from the men who had hold of him. Shouting—screaming—he ran like a madman down Rock Cut Road.

He didn't get more than forty or fifty feet before the first bullet slammed into his back. Next thing he knew, he was lying on his face, dirt in his mouth, more dirt in his nose. Something horrible was happening inside him. He felt on fire, only worse. When he tried to get up, he couldn't.

Big as a mountain, hard as a mountain, the deputy sheriff loomed over him. "All right, white boy," he ground out. "You coulda had it easy, same as your asshole buddies. Now we're gonna do it the hard way." He crouched down beside Price, grabbed his right arm, and broke it over his thigh like a broomstick. The sound the bones made when they snapped was just about like a breaking broomstick, too. The sound Cecil Price made . . . How the BKV men laughed!

With a grunt, the sheriff got to his feet. With the arrogant strut he always used, he walked around to Price's left side. With the coldblooded deliberation he'd shown before, he broke the white man's left arm. Price barely had room inside his head for any new torment.

Or so he thought, till one of the Black Knights of Voodoo kicked him in the crotch. "Ain't gonna mess with no black women now, are you, buckra?" he jeered. More boots thudded into Price's balls. That almost made him forget about his ruined arms. It *almost* made him forget about the bullet in his back, except he couldn't find breath enough to scream the way he wanted to.

After an eternity that probably lasted three or four minutes, the deputy sheriff said, "Reckon that's enough now. Let's finish him off and get rid of the bodies."

"I'll take care of it. Bet your sweet ass I will," Wayne Roberts said. He fired at Price again, and then again. Another gun barked, too, maybe once, maybe twice. By that time, Price had stopped paying close attention.

But he didn't fall straight into sweet blackness, the way Muhammad Shabazz and Tariq Abdul-Rashid had. He lingered in red torment when the BKV men picked him up and stuffed him into the trunk of one of their cars along with the Black Muslims' bodies.

The car jounced down the dirt road, every pothole and every rock a fresh stab of agony. At last, it stopped. "Here we go," somebody said as a Black Knight of Voodoo opened the trunk. "This ought to do the job."

"Oh, fuck, yes," somebody else said. Eager gloved hands hauled Cecil Price out of the trunk, and then the corpses of his friends.

"Hell, this dam'll hold a hundred of them." That was the deputy sheriff, sounding in charge of things as usual. "Go on, throw 'em in there, and we'll cover 'em up. Nobody'll ever find the sons of bitches."

Thump! That was one of the Black Muslims, going into a hollow in the ground. *Thump!* That was the other one. And *thump!* That was Cecil Price, landing on top of Tariq Abdul-Rashid and Muhammad Shabazz. An Everest of pain in what were already the Himalayas.

"Fire up the dozer," the deputy said. "Let's bury 'em and get on back to town. We done us a good night's work here, by God."

Somebody climbed up onto the bulldozer's seat. The big yellow Caterpillar D-4 belched and farted to life. It bit out a great chunk of dirt and, motor growling, poured it over the two

Black Muslims and Cecil Price. Price struggled hopelessly to breathe. More dirt thudded down on him, more and more.

Buried alive! he thought. *Sweet Jesus help me, I'm buried alive!* But not for long. The last thing he knew was the taste of earth filling his mouth.

HE WOKE IN DARKNESS, NOT KNOWING WHO HE WAS. THE TASTE of earth seemed to fill his mouth.

He sat bolt upright, gasping for breath, heart sledge-hammering in his chest as if he'd run a hundred miles. He looked around wildly. Tiny stripes of pale moonlight slipped between the slats of the Venetian blinds and stretched across the bedroom floor.

Beside him on the cheap, lumpy mattress, someone stirred: his wife. "You all right, Cecil?" she muttered drowsily.

A name! He had a name! He was Cecil, Cecil Price, Cecil Ray Price. Was he all right? That was a different question, a harder question. "I guess . . . I guess maybe I am," he said, wonder in his voice.

"Then settle down and go on back to sleep. *I* aim to, if you give me half a chance," his wife said. "What ails you, anyhow?"

"Bad dream," he answered, the way he always did. He'd never said a word about what kind of bad dream it was. Somehow, he didn't think he *could* say a word about what kind of bad dream it was. He'd tried two or three times, always with exactly zero luck. The words wouldn't form. The ideas behind the words wouldn't form, not so he could talk about them. But even if he couldn't, he knew what the dreams were all about. Oh, yes. He knew.

He still lived in the same brown clapboard house he'd lived in on that hot summer night in 1964, the brown clapboard house he'd lived in for going on forty years. It wasn't more than a block away from Philadelphia's town square.

He'd been Deputy Sheriff Cecil Price then. He ran for sheriff in '67, when Larry Rainey didn't go for another term, but another Klansman beat him out. Then he spent four years away, and after that he couldn't very well be a lawman any more. Once he came back to Mississippi, he worked as a surveyor. He drove a truck for an oil company. And he wound up a jeweler and watchmaker—he'd always been good with his hands. He turned into a big wheel among Mississippi Shriners.

But the dreams never went away. If he hadn't seen that damn Ford station wagon that afternoon . . . He had, though, and what happened next followed as inexorably as night followed day. Two Yankee busybodies: Michael Schwerner and Andrew Goodman. One uppity local nigger: James Chaney.

At the time, getting rid of them seemed the only sensible thing to do. He took care of it, with plenty of help from the Ku Klux Klan.

He wondered if the others, the ones who were still alive, had dreams like his. He'd tried to ask a couple of times, but he couldn't, any more than he could talk about his own. Maybe they'd tried to ask him, too. If they had, they hadn't had any luck, either.

Dreams. His started even before the damn informer tipped off the FBI about where the bodies were buried. At first, he figured they were just nerves. Who wouldn't have a case of the jitters after what he went through, when the whole country was trying to pull Neshoba County down around his ears?

Well, the whole country damn well did it. Back in June 1964, who would have dreamt a Mississippi jury—a jury of Mississippi white men—would, could, convict anybody for violating the civil rights of a coon and a couple of Jews? But the jury damn well did that, too. Price got six years, and served four of them in a federal prison in Minnesota before they turned him loose for good behavior.

He went on having the dreams up there.

Sometimes weeks went by when they let him alone, and he would wonder if he was free. And he would always hope he was, and he never would be. It was as if hoping he were free was enough all by itself for . . . something to show him he wasn't.

Did the dreams make him change? Did they just make him pretend to change? Even he couldn't say for sure. Ten years after he got convicted, he told a reporter—a New York City reporter, no less—he'd seen *Roots* and liked it. When he talked about integration, he said that was how things were going to be and that was all there was to it.

He spent years rebuilding his name, rebuilding his reputation. And then, in 1999, everything fell to pieces again. He got convicted of another felony. No guns this time, no cars racing down the highway in the heat of the night: he sold certifications for commercial driver's licensing without doing the testing he should have. A cheap little money-making scheme—except he got caught.

They didn't jug him that time. He drew three years' probation. But you could stay a hero—to some people—for doing what you thought you had to do to people who were trying to change the way of life you'd known since you were born. When you got busted for selling bogus certifications, you weren't a hero to anybody, even yourself. You were just a lousy little crook.

A lousy little crook with . . . dreams.

Two years later, a season after the turn of the century, he climbed up on a lift at an equipment-rental place in Philadelphia. He fell off somehow, and landed on his head. He died three days later at a hospital in Jackson—the same hospital where he'd brought the bodies of Schwerner and Goodman and Chaney for autopsy thirty-seven years earlier, after the FBI tore up the dam to get them out. He never knew that, but then, neither had they.

HE WOKE IN DARKNESS, NOT KNOWING WHO HE WAS. THE TASTE of earth filled his mouth.

THEY'D NEVER—

This one is Esther Friesner's fault. No one—and I mean no one—else could have come up with an anthology called *Alien Pregnant by Elvis*. Mashing tabloid reality, real reality (if there is such a thing), and science fiction together should be illegal. For all I know, it is. Nobody's busted me for it. Yet.

M ORT PFEIFFER SLUNG HIS JACKET OVER THE BACK OF HIS chair, then plomped his ample bottom into said chair and turned on his computer. *Another day*, he thought gloomily. He looked around the office of the *Weekly Intelligencer*.

It looked like a newspaper office: other people dressed no better than he was sat around in front of screens and clicked away at keyboards. Those clicks made it sound like a newspaper office, too. It even smelled like a newspaper office: stale coffee and musty air conditioning with two settings, too hot and too cold.

But it wasn't a newspaper office, or not exactly. If the *Intelligencer* wasn't the trashiest supermarket and 7-Eleven rack filler around, the troops hadn't done their job for the week. "For this I went to journalism school?" Mort muttered.

He wished for a cigarette. The smoke would have made the place smell even more authentic. But the *Intelligencer* office had gone smoke-free a couple of years before—it was either that or lose their health insurance. Besides, he was wearing a transdermal nicotine patch. Smoke while you had one of those things stuck to you and you were a coronary waiting to happen.

Behind glasses that were going to turn into bifocals the next time he got around to seeing his optometrist, his eyes lit up for a moment. Transdermal patches . . . he might be able to do something with that. They were hot these days, and no more than three percent of the lip-movers who bought the *Intelligencer* were likely to have even a clue about what *transdermal* meant.

So . . . the beginning of a headline formed in his mind, 72-point type, sans-serif, with an exclamation point at the end. TRANSDERMAL PATCHES CAUSE . . . !

"Cause what?" he mused aloud.

Cause heart attacks if you're stupid enough to keep lighting up while you're wearing one? He shook his head. That wasn't scary enough. You didn't necessarily die from a heart attack, and if you did, it was over quick.

Cause cancer? That one was stale even for the *Intelligencer* (which was saying something). Besides, the whole idea behind nicotine patches was to keep you from getting lung cancer. Pfeiffer's ethical sense was stunted (*Would I be here otherwise?* he thought), but it hadn't quite atrophied.

Cause AIDS? He shook his head again. Something there, though. Suddenly, like striking snakes, his hands leaped at the keyboard. Letters flowed rapidly across the screen: TRANSDERMALPATCHESCAUSEAIDS-LIKESYNDROME! He knew just how to write that one up. When you took the patch off, you went through some of the same whimwhams you did when you gave up smoking (he'd call a trained seal of a doctor for the impressive-sounding quotes he'd need). And some of those whimwhams were enough like early AIDS symptoms to give the piece the germ of truth his editor liked.

Speak of the devil, he thought, because his editor came by just then, paused to see what he was working on, and nodded approvingly before heading off to the next desk. Don't think of

Ed Asner as Lou Grant here. Katie Nelligan looked more like Mary Tyler Moore with red hair.

Mort sighed. If she hadn't been his boss, and if he hadn't had a well-founded suspicion that she was smarter than he was (although if she was all that smart, why did she work for the *Intelligencer*?), he'd have asked her out a year ago. *One of these days*, he kept telling himself. It hadn't happened yet.

Katie came back, dropped a wire service report into his IN basket. "See what you can do with this one, Mort," she said.

He looked at the news item. Kids in Japan, it seemed, raised stag beetles (not Japanese beetles, for some reason) as pets. Then they'd put them up on round cushions two at a time to see which one could grab the other by the projecting mouthparts and throw it off. They'd just chosen a national champion beetle.

"Jesus Christ," Mort said. "Sumo-wrestling bugs!"

"That's just the slant we'll want on it," Katie said. She nodded again—twice in one morning, which didn't happen every day. "Can you give me a draft before you go home tonight?"

"Yeah, I think so," he answered. What was he supposed to tell her?

"Good," she said crisply, and went on down the aisle between desks. Mort looked back at her for a couple of seconds before he returned to his computer.

He discovered he'd forgotten what he was going to write next about the transdermal patches. *No wonder*, he thought. Sumo-wrestling bugs—Lord, that was enough to derail anybody's train of thought. Bullshit about patches and the truth about bugs . . . "Hell of a way to make a living," he said under his breath.

Nobody glanced over at him to see why he was talking to himself. People at the *Intelligencer* did it ever day. Nobody, but nobody, was ever a bright-eyed, eager eighteen-year-old getting himself ready for a hot career writing for a supermarket tabloid. It wasn't a job you went looking for, it was a job you fell into— generally from a great height.

"If I weren't Typhoid Mary, I wouldn't be here," Mort said, again to himself. He'd worked for four different papers in three years, each of which went belly-up within months of hiring him. The jobs had disappeared, but his rent and his car payment and his child support hadn't. He'd been here five years. Whatever else you said about it, the *Intelligencer* wouldn't go broke any time soon. What was that line about nobody going broke overestimating the stupidity of the American people?

A guaranteed regular paycheck—yeah, that was one thing that kept him coming to the office every morning. The other was something he hadn't thought through when he'd taken this job: now that he'd worked for the *Intelligencer*, no *real* newspaper would ever take him seriously again.

He saved the patch story, got to work on the sumo-wrestling stag beetles. He took a certain perverse pride in the way he reworked it to fit the *Intelligencer*'s style: breezy, breathless, no paragraph more than two sentences long, no words more than three syllable if he could help it. Besides, Katie'd given him a deadline for that one, and he always met deadlines.

He was just heading into the wrapup when the lights went off.

"Oh, shit," he said loudly, an editorial comment echoed and embellished all over the office. When the lights went off, so did the computers. Mort hadn't saved the stag beetle story as he worked on it, so it was gone for good. He'd have to do it over from scratch, and doing it once had been once too often.

Besides which, with the power gone, the inside of the *Intelligencer* office was black as an IRS man's heart: no windows. The publisher, three floors up—he had a window, and one with an ocean view. The peons who did the actual work? They got peed on, as their name implied.

Katie Nelligan's voice cut through the chatter: "Does anybody have a flashlight at their desk? There's supposed to be an emergency kit in here somewhere, but we haven't needed it for so long, I've forgotten where."

No flashlights went on. Mort didn't even have a luminous watch. He just sat at his desk, figuring the only thing he was likely to do in pitch darkness was stumble over somebody's chair and break his fool neck.

Wouldn't that be a great way to go? If a network correspondent cut himself shaving while he was covering a war, he turned into a national hero overnight. But if a tabloid reporter killed himself trying to get out of his office, he might make page seven on the inside section of the newspaper. Having his passing altogether ignored was a hell of a lot more likely.

Somebody else did get up, and promptly tripped. Feeling smugly virtuous, Mort stayed put.

Then, all of a sudden, he could see again. Standing in the doorway were four slim, manlike shapes, each glowing a slightly different shade of bluish green. All together, they put out about as much light as a nightlight.

"Give me a break," Mort said. "Who's the practical joker?" Slim, glowing aliens were as much an *Intelligencer* hallmark as no funnies was with the *New York Times*. He'd written at least half a dozen stories about them himself. They all contradicted one another, but who kept track?

"I'll bet I know who did it," Katie Nelligan said: "San Levy at the *News of the World*." The *News of the World* specialized in aliens, too, generally warty yellow ones; Levy, who held down Katie's job over there, was a notorious prankster. Katie turned to the glowing quartet. "Okay, boys, you can knock it off now. We're wise to you. How about turning the lights back on, too?"

The four guys in the alien suits (Mort thought of them as John, Paul, George, and Ringo, which does a good job of dating *him*) didn't answer. One of them—George—started walking up toward the ceiling. There weren't any steps, but that didn't bother him. He just went up and up, as if the air were solid beneath his feet.

A couple of people broke into applause. "Hell of a special effect," someone called.

Mort gaped along with everybody else. It *was* a hell of a special effect. He would have been impressed seeing it on a movie screen. Seeing it for real, live and in person, was . . . unbelievable. You could put somebody in a suit that made him look like a freeway emergency light, yeah, but Mort knew for a fact that the ceiling didn't have any wires in it. Which left—what? Antigravity?

"Holy Jesus," he said hoarsely. "Maybe they *are* aliens."

The chorus of derision that brought down on his head couldn't have been louder or more scornful at an Air Force UFO debunking unit. People who worked for the *Intelligencer* wrote about aliens, sure, but they weren't dumb enough to believe in them. That was for the yahoos who bought the paper.

Then the fellow in the suit up by the ceiling pointed an (inhumanly?) long finger at Katie Nelligan. He didn't keep a flashlight in his fingernail, *à la* ET, but, with a startled squawk, Katie floated slowly off the floor and up toward him. "Somebody do something!" she yelped.

Mort sprang up, sprinted down the aisle, and grabbed her around the waist (he'd fantasized doing things like that, but not under these circumstances). He tried to pull her back down to mother earth. Instead, she rose higher and higher—and so did he.

He let go of Katie as soon as his feet left the ground, but that was too late. Up he went anyhow, toward the—well, if he wasn't an alien, he'd do until somebody showed up with Mars license plates.

About halfway to the ceiling, Mort remembered that once upon a time he'd been a pretty good reporter, and here he was, floating up to the biggest story in the history of mankind. "Get a camera!" he yelled at the top of his lungs. "We've got to have pictures!"

"Oh, good for you, Mort," Katie exclaimed. "God, we'll sell fifty million copies and we won't even have to make anything up." No matter that she'd been captured by aliens and was probably heading for a fate worse than taxes—she worried about the *Intelligencer*'s circulation ahead of her own.

Down on the ground, first one flash camera and then another started going off, strobing away until the office reminded Mort of nothing so much as a psychedelic '60s dance. Had the aliens smelled like pot smoke, the illusion would have been perfect, but they didn't smell like anything.

Only after he shouted for a camera did Mort stop to wonder whether the aliens would mind having their images immortalized in the *Intelligencer*. If they had minded, things might have turned decidedly unpleasant for the person on the wrong end of the Nikon. But they didn't seem to care one way or the other.

Then he wondered if anybody kept a gun in his desk or her purse. He didn't think the aliens would be able to ignore bullets like flash photography. If anybody was toting a piece, though, he didn't open up. That removed one of Mort's worries.

A bigger, more urgent one remained: now that the aliens had Katie and him, what would they do with them? The beings the *Intelligencer* featured were always looking out for humanity's best interests, but how likely was that really? Was a species that could invent pasteurized cheese food product worth saving anyhow? Mort had his doubts. Which left—what?

The first thing that sprang to mind was *experimental specimen*. That was a long walk off a short pier. Number two was *zoo specimen*. That might have its moments if they tried to establish a breeding population with him and Katie Nelligan, but in the long run it wasn't much better than number one: medium- to long-term insanity as opposed to instant anguish.

He flapped his arms and kicked his legs in midair, none of which changed his trajectory a bit. Whatever the aliens were going to do to him, he couldn't stop them.

His feet were still within grabbing distance of the ground, but when somebody—he didn't see who—made the same sort of run at him as he'd made at Katie, one of the aliens who'd remained by the doorway held up a hand like a traffic cop and his would-be rescuer bounced off an invisible wall. Pictures the aliens didn't mind; they wouldn't put up with anything more.

The one floating up by the ceiling—George—made a come-hither gesture to Mort and Katie, who duly went thither. The closer Mort looked at George, the less he looked like a human being, or even a *Star Trek* makeup job. For one thing, his head was too small. Making a head look bigger than it really is wasn't any great trick, but how did you go about shrinking one unless you were a South American Indian?

Nose, ears, mouth—details were all wrong: nothing you couldn't manage with makeup on any of them, maybe, but why would you? Besides those come-hither qualities, George's fingers had a couple of extra joints apiece. He had no nipples. Further down . . . well, Mort was damned if he'd let a makeup man do that sort of thing to *his* family jewels.

And if George wasn't an alien, what was he doing up here by the ceiling, and how had he got Katie and Mort up here with him? Mort's gut had needed a little while to catch up with his brain, but now he believed all over.

The alien extended the middle finger of his left hand toward him, the middle finger of his right toward Katie. Mort wanted to flip him off right back, but didn't have the nerve. George's finger touched the center of his forehead. He'd expected blazing heat. Instead, it was cool.

After that—the only person who understood what happened to him after that was Katie Nelligan, and only because it happened to her, too. He felt his brains getting systematically emptied and copied, as if he were a floppy being backed up onto an enormous hard disk. Everything he remembered, from the Pythagorean theorem to losing his cherry under the football stands in high school, got sucked up and flowed out through the alien's finger.

So did things he'd never imagined his brain retained: what he'd had for breakfast five years ago last Tuesday (two eggs over medium, wheat toast, grape jam, weak coffee); what his father had said when, sometime under the age of one, Mort spat up on the old man's best suit (not to be repeated here, but prime, believe me). *Amazing*, he thought, and hoped he'd keep one percent of what the alien was getting.

Even more amazing, though, was the backwash he got, as if a few random little documents from the hard disk snuck onto the floppy while the floppy played out onto the hard disk. Some of them came from Katie: the smell of her corsage on prom night, a sixth-grade spelling test where she'd missed the word *revolutionary*, what cramps felt like, and a long-distance call to her sister in Baltimore the spring before.

And some of those little documents had to come from George the alien: using those peculiar private parts in the manner for which they were intended, what felt like a college course on how flying saucers or whatever they were worked (which would have been worth a mint, and not a chocolate one, if Mort had understood the concepts), the taste of fancy alien food (by comparison, that ever-so-ordinary breakfast seemed nectar and ambrosia).

Mort also picked up a few impressions about what George thought of mankind. In two words, *not much*. He went about his job with all the enthusiasm of an Animal Regulations officer counting stray dogs around the city dump, except an Animal Regulations officer might actually like dogs.

The alien didn't like humans. Mort could think of a lot of reasons why benevolent aliens wouldn't like humans: they were busy polluting their planet; they fought wars; they discriminated on the basis of color, gender, sexual preference, and the size of your bankroll. If any of that had been in the backwash from George, Mort would have been chastened but not surprised.

It wasn't. George felt about humans much as a lot of nineteenth-century British imperialists had felt about the peoples they ruled: they were wogs. They were ugly, they smelled funny, they had revolting habits, and, most of all, they were *stupid*. George's view of what humans had in the brains department was somewhere between a badly trained dog and what that badly trained dog was liable to leave on your front lawn when it went out for a walk.

Given that George was currently pumping him and Katie dry of everything they'd ever known, Mort had to admit that, from his point of view, he had a point. But if George was a benevolent alien, he devoutly hoped he'd never run into one in a lousy mood.

All of a sudden, he was empty. The inside of his head seemed to be making the noise a soda straw does when you're still sucking but the soda's all gone.

A couple of more impressions backwashed into the sodaless expanse between his ears. One was a mental image of two scared-looking rubes in hunting gear getting the same treatment he was undergoing now. *I'll be damned*, he thought. *They weren't making it up after all.*

The second was a flash of alien mentation: *As long as we have to do it, this is the perfect spot for the survey. They'd never—* He never found out who *they* were or what they'd *never*. The document was incomplete.

George turned to his buddies by the door. He wiggled his ears. Mort didn't know what that meant, but the rest of the green-and-glowing Fab Four did: job's over for today. They went out the door. They didn't bother opening it first.

The floating alien looked from Mort to Katie and back again. Mort got the idea that if it had been up to him, he'd have dropped them both on the floor, ker*splat*. But maybe he had a supervisor watching him or something, because he didn't. He floated them down the same way they'd come up, only faster.

As they were descending, George went down the invisible stairs he'd gone up before. He left the *Intelligencer* office the same impossible way his colleagues had, except he left his nether cheeks on *this* side of the door for a couple of seconds while the rest of him was already on *that* side.

"Jesus," Mort said. "The moon from outer space."

Katie laughed—hysterically, sure, but can you blame her? Mort couldn't see what anybody else was doing, because the room was dark again now that the nightlights that walked like men had gone.

Then the lights came back on. It was as if that broke a spell; for all Mort knew, maybe it did. People started jumping and hollering and running to the door (but not through it) to find out if the aliens were still in sight. Mort didn't run to the door. Having seen the aliens more up close and personal than anybody but Katie Nelligan, he didn't want to see them again.

Katie said, "Whoever was taking those pictures, get them developed this instant, do you hear me? This instant! Don't leave the shop while they're being processed, either—wait for them right there."

That got three people out of the office. Mort glanced down at his watch, wondering how long he'd floated by the ceiling. What he saw made him blink and exclaim, "Katie, what time do you have?"

She looked at her watch, too, then stared at him, bright blue eyes wide with surprise. "It felt like we were up there for an hour, not a couple of minutes." She pointed to the wall clock. "But that says the same thing. Weird." She was not the sort of person to let weirdness overwhelm her; that was one of the reasons she was editor and Mort, older and arguably more experienced, just a staff writer. "We'll do drafts of the piece right now, while we still remember everything. When we're done, we'll compare notes. This one has to be *perfect*."

"Right." Mort all but sprinted for his computer. He'd never imagined being in the middle of a story like this. *Woodward and Bernstein, eat your hearts out*, he thought as he hit the keyboard.

He plunged in so hard and deep that he started violently when Katie tapped him on the shoulder. "I just wanted to say thanks," she told him. "That was brave, what you did."

"Oh. That. Yeah. Sure," he said. "Listen, why aren't you writing?" Katie laughed softly and went away.

THE NEXT THING MORT REMEMBERED APART FROM WORDS flowing from his mind to the computer was the pictures coming back. For that he was willing to get up from his desk. He'd expected something would go wrong—they'd be fogged, or black, or something. But they weren't. There was the alien, doing the mind-probe on him and Katie while all three of them floated in midair. There were the other aliens by the door. Shot after perfect shot—it was just a matter of picking the best ones.

"We've got 'em," Katie said. Everybody nodded.

Five o'clock came and went. Mort never noticed. Neither did Katie. Finally, at about half past six, she printed her story. Mort said, "I'll be done in just a few minutes." He pulled his sheets out of the laser printer when he was through, then said, "We both must have run way long. Shall we"—he hesitated, then plunged—"compare and cut over dinner?"

She gave him not the wary, thoughtful look he'd expected, but a sidelong glance and half a smile, as if she knew something he didn't. "All right," she said. "Let's go to Napoli. It's right down the street, and we have a lot of work to do to get this the way it has to be."

They went through each other's stories alongside lasagna and Chianti. Time on real newspapers had made Mort sharp at writing lean and tight; he boiled away a quarter of Katie's piece without touching the meaning at all.

She attacked his differently, looking more at what it said than how it did the saying. About halfway through, she looked up and said, "Backwash? That's a good way to put it. I felt it, too. I wondered if you had. But somebody reading the piece is going to need more explanation than you've given it here." She scribbled a note in the margin.

Over spumoni ("To hell with the waistline; today I earned it," Katie said), each looked at what the other had done. Most of Katie's comments asked for more detail here, less there, and made Mort's story more tightly focused and coherent. He tipped the cap he wasn't wearing. "Thanks. This'll help."

"I like what you've done with mine, too," she answered. "It's a lot crisper than it was. We make a pretty good team."

"Yeah." Mort beamed. He'd had just enough wine to improve his attitude, not enough to hurt his thinking.

Katie dabbed at her lips with a napkin. "Now let's get back to the office and hammer 'em together."

Mort almost squawked, but he didn't. What did he have to go home to? An empty apartment and celebrity dog wrestling on ESPN? Real work, important work (something he'd never imagined at the *Intelligencer* till now) was more important than that, and the company better. He took out his wallet, tossed bills on the red-and-white checked tablecloth, got to his feet. "Let's go."

"Hey, I was going to pay for mine," Katie said.

He shrugged. "I'm not broke, and I'm not trying to take advantage of you. If you want to buy for both of us one of these days, I'll let you."

She gave him that funny sidelong look again, but rose from the table without saying anything more. The night watchman scratched his head when they went back to the *Intelligencer* office. "You folks don't usually work late."

"Big story—a real 'Hey, Martha!' " Katie said solemnly.

"Yeah?" The watchman's eyes lit up. "Does it have Madonna in it?" When Mort and Katie both shook their heads, his shoulders slumped in disappointment. "How can it be a big story if it don't have Madonna in it?"

They went inside without answering, then settled down to

work side by side. A couple of hours later, sheets slid into the laser printer tray, one after the other. Mort scooped them up, saying, "Let me go over these one more time. I've been using a computer for ten years now, but I still edit better on hard copy."

"Yeah, me too." Katie read over his shoulder. They each made a last few changes, then printed out the altered pages again. This time Katie took them from the printer. She slid them into their proper places, made a neat little pile of the story, and stuck a paper clip in the top left corner. "It's done."

"Wait," Mort said. "Let me have it for a second." He took it over to the xerox machine, made two copies. "I'll take one of these home, and I'll stash the other one in my desk—just in case."

"In case the aliens come back, you mean?" Katie said. He nodded. She went on, "I don't think it'd help, but it can't hurt, either. First thing tomorrow, I go upstairs and lay this"—she hefted her own copy of what they'd done "—and the photos on Mr. Comstock. If he says no, I quit."

"Me, too," Mort said. Some things, by God, *were* more important than a job.

Katie yawned. "Let's go home. It's been a long day."

"Boy, hasn't it just?"

Everyone in the *Intelligencer* office stared nervously at the door through which the aliens had departed. Mort wasn't anticipating their return; like the rest of the tabloid crew, he was waiting for Katie Nelligan to come back from her conference with the publisher. She'd been up there a long time.

The door opened, which proved it wasn't the aliens coming back. Everybody jumped all the same. In stamped Katie, looking the way a Fury might have if she were Irish instead of classical Greek.

Mort could find only one reason for her to look like that. "Mr. Comstock won't go for it?" he exclaimed in dismay.

"Oh, no. He will. We lead with it, next week's issue." Katie bit off the words one by one. Little spots of color that had nothing to do with rouge rode high on her cheeks. "But he doesn't believe it. He doesn't believe us."

Cries of outrage echoed from walls and ceilings. "What does he think, we made it up to sell his stinking papers?" Mort yelled. "We'll all go up there and tell him—"

"No we won't. I told him the same thing, and he said we'd regret it if we tried." Katie's scowl grew darker. "And yes, that's just what he thinks. On the photos, he thinks he spotted the wires holding us up in the air."

"Jesus!" If he hadn't already been starting to bald, Mort would have torn his hair. "There weren't any goddamn wires!" The memory of yesterday's terror flooded back, sharp as a slap in the face.

"I know that as well as you do, Mort," Katie said. "So here's what I've got in mind: we're going to pretend we don't care what Mr. Comstock says. We'll put this out the right way, and people *will* believe it."

The staff sprang to work with the fire and dedication mutiny can call forth. They threw themselves at the story with the dogged, fatalistic courage of English infantry climbing out of their trenches and marching into German machine-gun fire at the Somme. Mort was astonished at what some of the people—men and women whose total illiteracy he would till now have reckoned a boon to mankind—could do.

"You know, Katie," he said when the editor walked by, "this is gonna be a 'Hey, Martha!' to end all 'Hey, Marthas!' *Everybody* will want to read it."

"I think you're right. And we've got a real Freddie Krueger of a picture on the front page to grab 'em and pull 'em in." She bristled. "I had to stop Comstock from using the one that looked right up my skirt. That man!" She clenched her fists till the knuckles whitened.

Mort looked at his watch. It was getting close to five. "Do you want to drown your sorrows in another bottle of Chianti?" he asked.

She'll say no, he thought with the automatic pessimism of a man who'd been through a divorce and taken a few knocks afterwards for good measure. But she said yes. And after a truly Lucullan feast at Napoli (or Mort thought so, anyhow, but he was too happy to be objective), she went back to his apartment with him. The mess it was in proved he hadn't expected that. If it bothered her, she didn't let on.

Afterwards, still on the disbelieving side but happier—*much* happier—than he had been at the restaurant, he ran a hand down the smooth skin of her back and said, "What made you decide to—?" He let it hang there, so she could ignore it if she wanted to.

She gave him that I-know-something-you-don't-know look

again, the one he'd seen on her face when he asked her to dinner the day the aliens came. It stayed there long enough that he thought she wasn't going to answer. But she did, if obliquely: "Remember the backwash?"

"Huh?" he said, but then, realizing what she had to be talking about, he went on, "From the alien, you mean? Sure. What about it?"

Katie hesitated again, then said carefully, "I didn't mean just from the alien. Bits came from you, too, just like you got bits from me. And one of them happened to be . . . how you feel about me. It's hard to be sure about a man—I suppose it's hard for a man to be sure about a woman—but this time, I didn't need to have any doubts. And so—" She leaned forward on the rumpled bed and kissed him.

Absurdly, he was jealous. He'd gotten bits from her, sure, but nothing like that (as far as he was concerned, the prom corsage didn't count). The one he remembered most vividly had come from the alien, that contemptuous *They'd never* that broke off unfinished.

From what had happened since, Mort was beginning to think he knew who *they* were and what they'd *never*, but he didn't tell that to Katie. He might have been wrong—and even if he was right, what the hell could he do about it?

IF YOU WENT INTO A MARKET OR A CONVENIENCE STORE a few weeks ago, you probably saw the *Intelligencer* on its rack, jammed in there with the rest of the tabloids. You probably took a look at the front page photo, shook your head, and walked on by to get your beef jerky or pipe cleaners or whatever it was you needed.

And even if you plunked down your eighty-five cents and read the whole piece, odds are you just took it in stride. After all, a tabloid'd do anything to sell copies, right? *You'd never* believe in aliens, would you?

Katie cried when the story went belly-up. The late-night talk-show hosts didn't even take it seriously enough to make jokes about it. Mort wasn't surprised. The green-and-glowing guys had known just where to take their sample, all right.

But don't think this is a story without a happy ending. Mort and Katie are getting married next month. They still have a lot of planning to do, but they've agreed on one thing: the wedding won't be in the *Intelligencer*.

PUBLICATION HISTORY

"The Haunted Bicuspid"
Originally appeared in *The Enchanter Completed*, 2005.

"Reincarnation"
Originally appeared in *Amazing*, May 1990.

"The Phantom Tolbukhin"
Originally appeared in *Alternate Generals*, 1998.

"Moso"
Originally appeared in *Space and Time*, Summer 2008.

"Bluethroats"
Is original to this collection.

"Worlds Enough, and Time"
Originally appeared in *Analog*, January/February 2008.

"He Woke in Darkness"
Originally appeared in *Asimov's*, August 2005.

"They'd Never—"
Originally appeared in *Alien Pregnant by Elvis*, 1994.

This edition of 1000
(250 signed and limited/750 trade) hardcover copies
was printed by The Maple-Vail Book Manufacturing Group
on 55# Maple Antique paper
for WSFA Press in October 2009.

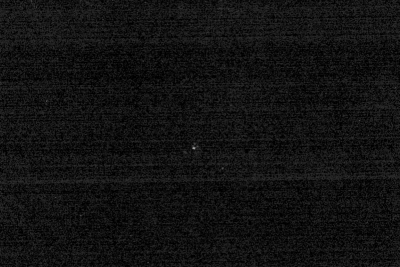